"It makes a delightful change to see you out of work clothes."

"Delightful? Isn't that taking courtesy a bit far?" she asked feverishly.

"Don't you like being described as 'delightful'?" Kane's eyes were shuttered. "What adjective would you rather I used? How about sexy? Mmm. Yes, sexy might be more apt. Those freckles, that ivory-white skin and flaming hair. Not obviously sexy, but discreetly so. Like a woman in jeans and a man's shirt, not thinking she's flaunting anything, but arousing all sorts of illicit thoughts anyway."

His words made her feel limp. "I don't arouse illicit thoughts," she squeaked.

"How do you know?"

NINE TO FIVE

*Getting down to business
in the boardroom…and the bedroom!*

A secret romance, a forbidden affair,
a thrilling attraction…

What happens when two people work together
and simply can't help falling in love—
no matter how hard they try to resist?

Find out in this series of stories
set against working backgrounds.

This month in

Secretary on Demand by Cathy Williams

As well as being Kane's secretary,
Shannon finds herself caring for his young
daughter—she even moves into his home! All the
while Shannon is fighting a powerful attraction
to her boss—until Kane dares her to act on it….

Cathy Williams

SECRETARY ON DEMAND

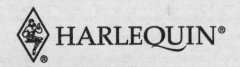

TORONTO • NEW YORK • LONDON
AMSTERDAM • PARIS • SYDNEY • HAMBURG
STOCKHOLM • ATHENS • TOKYO • MILAN • MADRID
PRAGUE • WARSAW • BUDAPEST • AUCKLAND

ISBN 0-373-12270-5

SECRETARY ON DEMAND

First North American Publication 2002.

Copyright © 2001 by Cathy Williams.

Visit us at www.eHarlequin.com

Printed in U.S.A.

CHAPTER ONE

'GUESS who's here, Shannon!'

Shannon paused for a second to look up at her friend who was contributing to the general chaos of the kitchens by balancing a large circular tray, laden with empty crockery, precariously above her shoulder on the flat of her hand.

'Who?' She flexed her fingers and grinned which was an open invitation for Sandy to deposit her tray on the stack of paperwork on the desk and lean forward with a conspirational gleam in her eyes. Sandy did amateur dramatics twice a week and devoutly believed that there was nothing in life that couldn't benefit from elaborate gestures. She would never make it to the big screen.

'Guess!'

'I would if I thought that Alfredo would let us get away with playing a few guessing games when it's pandemonium in here.' On cue, Alfredo yelled something threatening from across the kitchen and was blithely ignored. 'The Queen?' Shannon hazarded. 'A famous Hollywood star interested in sampling a more downmarket venue in fashionable Notting Hill? Someone from the Lottery Board coming to present you with a cheque for several million pounds?'

'*He's* here!' Sandy straightened up with a smug smile of satisfaction.

'What on earth is *he* doing here at this time of day?' Shannon felt a sudden little swell of excitement.

'Watch it, kid, you're going red in the face.'

'Who is he with?'

'No one. *At the moment...*' Sandy allowed the tantalising titbit to drop. 'But *he's requested two menus*!'

'We're sad people, Sandy.' Shannon stood up and smoothed down her calf-length black skirt. 'Wasting our time speculating on someone we don't know from Adam...' Which wasn't entirely true. They *did* know him, in a manner of speaking. The man had been coming in regularly to grace their eating establishment every morning, no later than seven, for months. In fact, almost as long as Shannon had been living in London, and there was a pleasurable familiarity about the routine.

Of course, they had both given in to wild speculation about him.

He was too aggressively good looking to ignore. His hair was very short and very dark and the sum total of his features added up to an impression of understated power that made their spectator sport of watching him virtually irresistible.

'Where are you going, my little Irish friend?' Sandy asked tartly. 'Don't you have a spot of important typing to be getting on with?'

'I'll just have a quick peek at him. See if he looks the same at lunchtime as he does first thing in the morning.'

'You mean you think that his mascara might have smudged? Lippy worn off a bit? Facial T-zones looking a bit greasy and in need of a dash of Almond Beige pressed powder?'

Shannon ignored her and quickly grabbed the cream and blue apron folded in the corner of her desk. She'd originally been hired as Alfredo's secretary, to look after his books, do his typing, take phone calls and generally make sure that the nuts and bolts of the restaurant were well oiled and running smoothly, but the plan had gone pear-shaped on day three when one of the waitresses had failed to show up and she'd been requisitioned to help serve tables. Since then, Shannon had combined her well-honed secretarial skills with her newly discovered waitressing talents, donning an apron whenever the situation demanded, and always in the morning when the paperwork could be left for a couple of hours.

By the time she had quickly slipped the apron over her head, Alfredo had appeared in all his five-feet-four, seriously corpulent Italian glory.

He was one of the few men in the entire world, Shannon was sure, whose lack of height made it possible for her to address him on an eye-to-eye level.

'Just taking over serving, Alfredo…' Shannon looked meaningfully at her friend who was hovering to one side like a spare part. 'Sandy's hurt her foot.'

'Don't you tell Alfredo anything about the hurt foots, missy! The foots looked just fine when she came a running over to whisper to you when it is madness here and I am not paying her to have the little cosy chats when she should be taking orders! Don't you two little missies think that Alfredo does not have the eyes at the back of the head! I see everything!'

The hurt foot had been a good idea. It released Sandy's barely contained lust for drama and she instantly shot into wounded mode, removing one shoe and tenderly touching her ankle as though it might explode at any minute if too much pressure was applied.

Shannon took the opportunity to scuttle through the kitchen, pausing to glance at the orders stacked on the counter, then hustled outside into the restaurant.

Yes, so what if she was sad? A sad twenty-five-year-old girl who had fled Ireland in a welter of misery and had grasped at the giggling normality of fantasising about a mysterious customer who had fired her imagination. Didn't her imagination deserve to be fired after what she had been through? It was all a silly game but silly games had been just what her depressed soul had needed.

She walked briskly over to his table and appeared to be startled at finding him there.

If she had been Sandy, she would have been far more elaborate when it came to playing startled. Instead, she smiled with consummate politeness and said, 'Oh! What a pleasant surprise to see you here at lunchtime, sir! Shall I take your order or are you waiting for someone?'

'Oh! And what a pleasant surprise, seeing *you* at lunchtime, and, yes, you may take my order for a drink but I am waiting for someone.'

He had a deep, slow voice that had a disturbing tendency to curl around her nervous system, which was what it was doing now. He leaned back in his chair and looked at her with amusement.

'I thought your little blonde friend was serving me.'

'Oh, Sandy's hurt her ankle. She's sitting for a few minutes.'

'In that case, I'll have a bottle of the Sancerre. Could you make sure that there's ice in my glass? I like my white wine very cold.'

'Of course, sir. Will that be all?'

'Now, there's a leading question,' he murmured, and Shannon's colour rose. *Was he flirting?* No. Impossible. The man might be terrifyingly good-looking but he was also highly conventional. Didn't he wear impeccably tailored suits and read the *Financial Times* every morning?

She cleared her throat and met his dark eyes steadily. 'Perhaps I could bring you a little appetiser to sample while you wait for your friend? One of our chefs has prepared some delicious crab and prawn pastries.'

'Tempting.'

'Or you could wait until your partner arrives.'

'My partner?' he drawled with lazy amusement. 'In what context would you be using the word "partner"?'

Shannon looked at him in confusion. She'd assumed that his lunch date was with a woman. Maybe even his wife, although he didn't wear a wedding ring. Or maybe, she thought sheepishly, she had just been fishing for information.

'You blush very easily. Has anyone ever told you that? And when you blush, you look even more like a schoolgirl, especially with those braids on either side. What sort of partner do you think I'm meeting for lunch? A female partner, perhaps?'

'I'm very sorry, sir. I just assumed...perhaps your wife...or maybe a female friend...'

'I don't have a wife, actually, and *a female friend...*' He let his voice linger on the description for a few seconds while he continued to watch her gravely. 'What an extraordinarily quaint way of putting it. Alas, though, no female friend on the scene either.'

Her surprise must have registered on her face because he laughed softly and raised his eyebrows. 'Yes, I'm one of those sad old men who is still waiting for the right woman to come along and make an honest man of him.' Disconcertingly, the mildness in his voice seemed to encourage a response to this, but for the life of her Shannon couldn't think of a thing to say. She got the distinct impression, in fact, that the man was trying to tease her.

'I'm sure that's not the case,' she replied tartly, shoving the order pad into the pocket of her apron and doing something pointless with the cutlery on the table because she was rather enjoying the feeling of being watched by those incredible eyes.

'What makes you say that?'

'If that will be all, sir, I'll just go and fetch your wine.'

'You mean you're leaving me in the middle of my unanswered question?'

'I'm very busy at the moment, sir.' She drew herself up to her full height of five feet three and looked down at the darkly amused face. 'I'll return with your drinks order...'

'And some of the delicious crab and prawn pastries...'

'What? Oh, yes. Right.'

It was the strangest conversation she'd had with him since he'd appeared through the door months earlier and she found that she was shaking when she returned to the kitchens. Let that be a lesson to her not to indulge her curiosity! She'd been bitten by the speculation bug and he'd returned the favour with panache, deliberately playing verbal games with an air of complete fake gallantry. She would be better off getting back to the work she was paid to do.

'Your foot's completely better,' she informed Sandy, when she managed to eventually corner her, 'and table four wants a bottle of Sancerre. A bucket of ice on the table as well.'

'Oh, dear. I take it your curiosity has been satisfied?'

'The man,' Shannon said loftily, 'is not quite the paragon of politeness we thought he was.'

Sandy's eyes gleamed with sudden alertness. 'Ooh... Tell me more... Was he rude?'

'No.' Shannon sat down and rustled lots of paper into a stack then she pushed a button on her computer so that the screen lit up. How was she supposed to get any work done when her desk was stuck here off the end of the kitchens without even a partition to separate one from the other? It was noisy and disorienting and she felt giddy.

'Oh. Did he make a pass at you, then?'

Shannon's eyes shot to her friend's with horror. 'He most certainly did not!' she denied vehemently.

'Then what did the man do?'

'He…he… Nothing really, I suppose,' she said lamely. 'But you can carry on serving him, and you'd better hurry with his wine before he marches in here to find out what's going on. Oh, and he wants some of those crabby pastry things as well.'

She would take no further interest in him, or his lunch companion for that matter.

So when, ten minutes later, Alfredo announced to her that she would have to help out with the serving, she point-blank refused. Albeit in a pleading tone of voice and sheltering behind the excuse of having to catch up on her paperwork.

'Are you disobeying me, missy?' Alfredo's jowls wobbled and he folded his arms expressively. He had an array of menacing gestures which routinely failed to work because his jolly approach to life was always too near the surface. He was a sucker for giving leftovers to their little coterie of down-and-outs who stopped by every night at closing time and sometimes he would force them to comment on some of his concoctions. How could anyone resist Alfredo?

Which was why Shannon ended up sticking on the apron again with a little sigh of frustration. As luck would have it, table four needed their order. She decided that it would be good practice at smiling brightly and acting like a sophisticated Londoner who could handle most things without batting an eyelid, which was the image she was steadily trying to create. On no account would she allow the man, still nameless, to think that he had thrown her into a tizzy with his word games.

She approached his table with the plates, studiously avoiding eye contact, and gently deposited the halibut in front of him. Then she decided to further test her *savoir-faire* by asking him whether his wine was all right.

'Enough ice, sir?'

'A bucket is more than enough,' he agreed in a murmur. 'And the little crab pastries were truly exquisite. My compliments to the chef.'

'I'll pass on the message,' Shannon said, rather proud at her self-containment.

'Very obliging of you.' He looked at his food and she had a sneaking suspicion that there was something resembling a smile lurking at the corners of his mouth.

She turned to his companion and the practised smile froze. She could feel the colour drain away from her face.

'You!' she whispered, clutching the plate of food. 'What are *you* doing here!' Her fragile mastery over her emotions crumbled spectacularly away in the face of Eric Gallway, who was sitting back in his chair, looking at her with smiling, polite blankness. He was as blond-haired and blue-eyed as she remembered, with the plastic good looks of someone who had spent a lifetime cultivating their outward image to the detriment of everything else. He'd captured her with his looks and then used every ounce of smooth charm at his disposal to try and get her into bed with him. Goodness knew, he might have succeeded as well in the end if she hadn't found out about his wife and his children and the whole life he had conveniently concealed while promising her happy-ever-afters and wedded bliss. Only then had he turned vicious and the mask had slipped away to reveal a small man with a nasty, cruel mind.

'Excuse me, do I know you, miss?'

In retrospect, it was the worst thing he could have said. In retrospect, Shannon liked to think that she wouldn't have done what she had if he'd acknowledged her. Looking at her coolly and blankly and pretending that he didn't have a clue who she was, it sent all the vanished colour rushing back into her cheeks. Her frozen hands began to tremble with rage.

'Maybe you don't. How disappointing,' she agreed. She heard her mother's voice telling her to always count to ten because her temper would get her into trouble one day, and made it to two before she removed the plate from the tray and tipped twelve ounces of medium-rare steak, dripping with Alfredo's special sauce, accompanied by potatoes and vegetables, straight onto the pristine jacket and well-tailored trousers.

It was intensely satisfying to hear Eric Gallway's yelp of pain as hot food hit the thin covering of expensive wool. It reverberated through the restaurant like the crash of breaking crockery in a china shop. He stood up and frantically began wiping the food with his napkin, while everyone in the restaurant stopped eating and positioned themselves the better to look at what was going on.

'How dare you?' he growled. 'How *dare* you throw a plate of food over me? I don't know who the hell you are, miss, but I'm damn well going to make sure you're sacked! Get me your boss! This instant!'

Shannon had a strong urge to laugh and covered her mouth with her hand. No need to get her boss. Alfredo was hurrying over towards them while trying to encourage the other diners to carry on with their meals. Perhaps pretend that this was nothing but some simple Italian jollity.

'What is going on here?' Alfredo ignored Eric's frantic cleaning-up process and stared at Shannon who hung her head. Hopefully, he would interpret that as a gesture of shame instead of an insane desire to stifle her mirth.

'What,' snarled Eric, 'do you think the problem is? This…this…*so-called* waitress of yours has dumped a plate of food all over me and let me tell you right now that unless she's sacked immediately, I'll sue you for everything you possess! I'll personally make sure that this restaurant is out of business!'

'It sort of fell, the plate,' Shannon said, her green eyes wide and luminous. If he could pretend not to know who the hell she was, then she could pretend that it had all been an unfortunate accident. 'Sorry.' She grabbed a serviette and made a flicking motion, which was venomously brushed aside. 'I think some of the carrots oozed into your pocket, *sir*…and there are a few mange-tout on your left shoe…'

Eric seemed incapable of responding to the helpful observations and stared at her murderously as Alfredo launched into a profuse apology, ending with assurances that any dry-cleaning costs would be covered.

'Oh, dear, your lovely patent leather shoes seem to be ruined,' Shannon observed with extravagant seriousness.

'Please, allow me to offer you a full replacement for your suit and your shoes.' All eyes followed a path down the soaked trousers to the ruined shoes under discussion. Someone burst out laughing a few tables away.

'You sack this *creature* immediately, my man, or you won't be able to afford your next loaf of bread, never mind my clothes. And let me tell you something, I happen to know quite a number of people in high places!'

'I think it's time you took yourself off to the bathroom and cleaned up,' drawled a familiar voice. 'You're making a spectacle of yourself.'

For a minute, Eric looked as though, now in his stride and regardless of the state of his clothes, he was more than prepared to stand his ground and continue his litany of threats, but after a few seconds he nodded and walked off, watched by everyone in the restaurant. Someone yelled for an encore and Shannon felt a rush of appreciation for the bawdy clientele who frequented their establishment.

'I hope your friend will calm down,' Alfredo began worriedly. 'Of course, it was a dreadful accident, but all these threats of closing down my restaurant...well, I have a family to support! Perhaps I better go see what is happening in the bathroom, hope he listens to reason...' He extracted a handkerchief from a pocket to wipe his brow and then hurried off towards the direction of the bathroom.

'Sit down.'

Shannon slowly turned to look at the man, who seemed to be the only person in the restaurant unaffected by what had just taken place.

She slumped into a free chair and rested her head against her hands.

'Feel better?'

She looked at him for a while in silence. 'Not really, no, but thank you for asking.'

'What was that all about?'

'I'm very, very sorry that I ruined your lunch.' She stared at the congealing halibut on his plate. There was nothing funny about what had just happened, she realised. Alfredo had had nothing to do with anything, but he had taken the brunt of it and it had all been her fault.

'Forget the lunch,' he said drily.

'Poor Alfredo,' she said miserably to herself. 'I shouldn't have dropped the plate of food all over your friend. It was wrong of me.'

'He's not my friend. You certainly know how to create a scene, don't you?'

'Were you very embarrassed? I'm very, very sorry.'

'Will you stop apologising? And, no, I wasn't embarrassed. It would take rather more than that little incident to embarrass me. Tell me what you're going to do now.'

'Resign, of course.' She stood up and his eyes followed her thoughtfully. 'What choice do I have? Alfredo will never trust me with another plate of food, and I couldn't blame him. Who needs a waitress with a talent for flinging food over customers?' Besides, she *knew* Eric Gallway and she knew that he was more than capable of doing his utmost to get what he would see as just revenge for his humiliation.

'Resign, reds? And who will serve me my morning coffee and bagel?'

He was trying to be nice. In the midst of her misery, she realised that he had called her 'reds', a reference, she assumed, to her bright red hair, and the softly spoken intimacy was almost as powerfully unsettling as the prospect of her future without a job.

'I'm going to pack up my things,' she said glumly. 'Thanks for being so understanding.' She reached out to shake his hand, for some unknown reason, but instead of a shake, he casually linked his fingers through hers and squeezed her hand gently, then he reached for his glass of wine and sipped some, with his fingers still interlinked with hers. He rubbed his thumb idly against hers and she felt a curious sensation of prickling down the back of her neck. Then he released her.

'I don't suppose you'd like your meal replaced?' she joked half-heartedly, and he raised his eyebrows, appreciating her attempt at humour.

Funny, during all their speculations about him, she had never noticed how strongly the curves of his mouth spoke of compassion and humour. Or maybe anyone would have seemed compassionate and humorous alongside Eric with his infernal vanity and monstrous self-absorption.

'Strangely, I appear to have lost my appetite.' He gave her a little half-smile.

'Well.' She heaved a sigh. 'The halibut was very good. Trust me. Much better than the wretched steak.'

She walked the long walk back to the kitchens, and by the time she'd told Alfredo she was resigning, said her last goodbyes to everyone and cleared her desk of what belonged to her, her usual buoyancy was back with her.

She would find something else. She wasn't fussy. Hadn't she ended up enjoying Alfredo's even though initially the early start had put her off and the hours were often longer than her contract demanded? She would find something else and she would enjoy it. And if she didn't, then couldn't she always head back up to Dublin?

True, it felt good to be away from the claustrophobia of having all her large family around her but if she did decide to go back to Ireland, she knew that she would settle back in without any real difficulty. And after all this time, they would have at least stopped oozing sympathy about her wrecked love life and making endless remarks about adulterous men and young, impressionable girls.

Things would work out. She had a sudden, wild memory of the man with his fingers entwined with hers and felt a little shiver of regret. One face lost to her for ever. For no reason whatsoever, the thought depressed her, and she was so busy trying to analyse the foolishness of her reaction that she didn't notice him until he was standing in front of her. Towering over her, in fact. Shannon just manage to stop before she collided with his immovable force and it was only when her eyes actually trailed upwards that she recognised him and gave a little gasp of surprise. Mostly because he seemed to have materialised from the sheer power of the thoughts in her head.

'How did it go?'

'What are you doing here?' She wanted to reach out and prod him to see if he was real.

'Waiting for you, as a matter of fact.'

'Waiting for me? Why would you be waiting for me?' It wasn't yet four-thirty, but the light was already beginning to fade and there was an unholy chill in the autumn air.

'To make sure that you were all right.'

'Of course I'm all right.' She stuck her hands in her pockets and stared at his shoes. She hadn't realised how big a man he was. Not just tall, but broad-shouldered and powerfully built. 'Why shouldn't I be?' She raised her eyes to his and made fleeting contact.

'Because, reds, you looked pretty shaken up back there in the restaurant.'

Shannon debated whether she should tell him to stop calling her 'reds' and decided, perversely, that she liked the nickname.

'Did I?' she said airily. 'I thought I handled myself very well, actually. I mean, losing a job isn't the end of the world, is it?' Bills. Rent. Food. Not the end of the world but not far off.'

'Look, it's cold trying to hold a conversation out here. Why don't you hop in my car. I want to talk to you.'

'*Hop in your car?* I'm very sorry but I can't do that.'

'Why not?'

'Because I don't know you. You could be anyone. Don't get me wrong. I'm not saying you're an axe-wielding maniac, but you *could* be for all I know.'

'An axe-wielding maniac?' he asked, bemused.

'Or a fugitive from the law. Anyway, my mother told me never to accept lifts from strangers.'

'I'm not a stranger! You've been serving me breakfast every morning just about for months! Nor am I a fugitive from the law. If I were a fugitive from the law, wouldn't I be hiding out somewhere less conspicuous than a busy Italian restaurant in the middle of crowded Notting Hill? Your imagination is obviously as vivid as your temper, reds.'

'And stop calling me *reds*.' She'd decided she didn't care for the appellation after all. It was insulting.

'Then accompany me, please, for a short ride in my car which is just around the corner. I want to talk to you.'

'Talk about what?'

'Oh, good grief,' he groaned. 'Let me put it this way, it'll be worth your while.' He turned on his heel and began walking away, expecting her to follow him, and she did, clutching her coat around her and half running to keep up.

'I don't even know your name!' she panted in his wake. 'And where are you planning on taking me for this little talk that will be worth my while?'

He stopped abruptly and she cannoned into him. Instinctively he reached out and steadied her. 'Kane Lindley,' he said, 'in answer to your first question. And a little coffee-bar two blocks away in answer to your last. We could walk but my time on the meter is about to run out so it's as easy for us to take the car and I'll find somewhere else to park.'

She realised that he was still holding her by her arms, and he must have realised that as well because he politely dropped his hands and waited for her to respond.

'Kane Lindley…'

'That's right. Have you heard of me?'

'Why should I have heard of you?' Shannon asked, puzzled.

He said swiftly, 'Absolutely no reason. I'm not a celebrity but I own Lindley publications and I'm now in charge of a television network.' He zapped open his car with his remote after a short mental tussle. Shannon hurried over to the passenger side and slipped in, slamming the door against the stiff cold.

'I haven't heard of Lindley publications,' she told him as soon as he was sitting next to her.

'It doesn't matter.' His voice was irritable. 'I'm not trying to impress you. I'm merely trying to put you at ease in case you think I'm not to be trusted.'

'Oh. Right. Well…' She stared out of the window. 'I'm Shannon McKee. How long were you lurking around, waiting for me to come out, anyway?'

'I wasn't lurking around, reds,' he growled. 'As a matter of fact, I went to buy some ties at a little shop tucked away around the corner and then dropped back here. Coincidentally, you were leaving.'

The coffee-bar really was only a couple of streets away and they got a parking space instantly. It felt kind of nice to be the one sitting at the table and being waited on for a change. Meals out had been few and far between since she'd moved down to London, where the cost of living had hit her for six and relaxed cups of coffee in trendy coffee-bars, as this one was, had been even more of a rarity.

He ordered a cafetière of coffee for two and a plate of pastries and then proceeded to look at her with dark-eyed speculation. 'Now, tell me a little about yourself. I know you don't like football, like the theatre even though you never get there, loathe all exercise except swimming and are self-conscious about your hair, but what are you doing in London?'

Shannon blushed. She never would have guessed that her passing titbits of information had been stored away. She would have assumed that he had more important things to think about than the details of a waitress's life. 'I am not self-conscious about my hair!' she snapped, a little disconcerted by this regurgitation of facts.

'Then why you do always wear it tied back?'

'Because it's convenient. And I'm in London because...because I wanted a change from Ireland. I lived in a little village about twenty miles outside Dublin and I guess I wanted to sample something a little different.' Now that he had mentioned her wretched hair, she found that she couldn't stop fiddling with it, tugging the ends of the braids. She had to force herself to fold her hands neatly on her lap.

'I wish you'd stop looking at me,' she said after a while. Here they were, one to one, no longer in the roles of waitress serving customer, and their sudden equality made her feel breathless. She felt as though those un-readable, considering eyes could see straight past the dross and into all the secret corners of her mind that she preferred not to share with anyone.

'Why? Does it make you feel uncomfortable?' He didn't labour the point, though. Thankfully. Instead, once their coffee and pastries were in front of them, he began asking her about her work experience and what she had done in Ireland and what she had done since moving to London, tilting his head to one side as she rambled on about her education and her first job and her secretarial qualifications.

'So,' he said finally, 'you did secretarial work, but really you'd call yourself quite adaptable.'

'I can turn my hand to most things.'

'I'll get to the point, reds. Sorry, Miss McKee. I feel very badly about what happened today. I've been coming to Alfredo's for months and I know that you're good at what you do. I suspect you enjoyed working there and the fact is that if I hadn't chosen to go there at lunchtime with that particular person, you would not now be out of a job.'

'It's not your fault.'

Kane relaxed back and folded his arms. 'That's as maybe, but the fact remains that I would like to make amends by offering you a job…working for…me.'

CHAPTER TWO

'YOU want me *to work for you*?' Shannon asked incredulously. 'But you don't know me! Not really! You don't even have any references! You've seen me wait tables at Alfredo's for a few months, and we've chatted off and now, and now you're offering me a job as your secretary because *you feel obligated*?' Her eyes dropped from Kane's face to his big hands, cradling the sides of his mug. Somehow the thought of working for this man frankly terrified her.

'And are you qualified to throw job offers around willy-nilly?' she pressed on, frowning. 'What will your boss say?'

'I *am* the boss. I own the company, lock, stock and barrel. I told you that already. Everyone in the company reports to me, reds.'

'I told you to stop calling me by that name,' Shannon said absent-mindedly. 'Anyway, aren't there more suitable candidates lining up for the job? And how come you've coincidentally got a position vacant?' She chewed her lip, mulling over this wildly improbable development and trying to read between the lines to the hidden agenda. Because there must be a hidden agenda. Job offers involved interviews and references and procedures. They didn't land like ripe plums into your lap without there being one or two glaring catches.

'I mean, top executives are never without a secretary. Someone is always available to handle things like that, to make sure that vacant positions get filled.' If he

owned the company, he need only snap fingers and there
would be someone on the scene, saluting and racing off
to make sure that a suitable secretary was located pronto.
He wouldn't be lounging around, making do on the
offchance that someone might show up at some point in
time.

'Oh, dear. In that case, perhaps I'm lying. Perhaps I
don't own Lindley publications after all.' He laughed
with genuine amusement and gave her a long, leisurely
and far too all-encompassing a look for her liking.
'Don't worry, reds, you're asking all the right questions.
The job exists because my old secretary retired to live
in Dorset with her widowed sister two months ago and
since then I've been using a selection of secretaries, none
of whom has been particularly suitable. My only alternative at the moment is to usurp one of my director's
personal assistants who *would* be able to cope with the
workload, but it's not an ideal choice because it would
entail leaving someone else facing the same problem.
Aside from that obvious problem, there are one or two
other considerations that need to be met, and I assure
you, not that I need to, that the lady in question would
be unable to meet them.'

As far as Shannon was concerned, the situation was
getting more and more bizarre by the moment. 'What
other considerations?' she asked slowly. She nibbled one
of the pastries and looked at him steadily as she did so.

'Before we get to those, just tell me whether or not
you're interested in the job.'

'Naturally, I'm interested in getting *a* job. Having just
been forced into early retirement from the last one.'

'Well, shall we skip the arguments for the moment so
that I can try and establish what sort of secretarial experience you possess? Obviously, if your experience is

insufficient, you can be slotted in somewhere a bit lower down the scale, although working for me is more than a matter of relevant secretarial experience. I'm looking for an attitude and I think you've got it.'

'Because I've been so successful as a waitress? Except for today when I flung a plate of hot food over a customer?'

'I particularly liked the way you pointed out the stray mange-tout he had missed on his shoe.' He gave her a crooked smile, then before she could respond he leaned forward and casually brushed the side of her mouth with his finger. 'Pastry crumbs,' he murmured. 'So, run your background by me.'

'All right. What do you want to know?' She had to clasp her hands very tightly together to stop herself from touching the spot where his finger had been.

'A brief job history would be nice. Details of what your actual jobs involved.'

'School, secretarial college, several temporary positions and then, for the past three years, a permanent job working for a radio station just outside Dublin. A local radio station that focused on good music and gossip. Generally speaking, I did all the office work and also updated their computer programs to accommodate their growth. They were in a bit of an administrative mess when I arrived, actually, so it was a challenge to get things straight. It was a fantastic job,' she added wistfully. 'Never a dull moment and the people there were great fun.'

'So, bored with the personal satisfaction of it all, you decided to leave…'

'Not quite.'

'Then why did you leave?' He looked at her evenly. 'I'm not asking out of morbid curiosity, but as your potential employer I have to establish whether your abrupt departure might influence my decision. I mean, did you leave for the pay?'

'I left...for personal reasons,' she said, flushing. Passing conversations with him had not prepared her for his tenacity.

'Which might be...what?'

'I don't see that that's relevant.'

'Of course it's relevant.' He drained his cup of coffee. 'What if you left for the personal reason of, let's say, theft?'

'Theft!'

'Or...flamboyant insubordination. Or immoral conduct...'

Shannon burst out laughing. 'Immoral conduct? Oh, please! What kind of immoral conduct?'

'Stripping at the office party? Smoking on the premises? Sex in the boss's office when there was no one around?' His voice was mild, so why did she suddenly feel her skin begin to prickle? She imagined herself lying on a desk in his office, with those long fingers touching every part of her body, and she shrank back in shaken horror from the image. It had been as forceful as it had been unexpected.

'I have all my references back at my bedsit,' she told him primly.

'At your *bedsit*?'

'Correct.'

'You *live* in a bedsit?'

'It's all I could afford. Anyway...' she paused and reluctantly flashed him a wry smile '...a bedsit is the height of luxury after you've grown up in a house with seven siblings.'

'You have...' He looked green at the thought of it.

Hates children, she thought smugly, perversely pleased that she had managed to shake some of that formidable self-control. Probably an only child. She and Sandy had never actually speculated on his family background but she would have bet money that he was the cosseted son of doting parents who had given in to his every whim, hence his unspoken assumption that he could get whatever he wanted at the click of a finger.

'I know. That's how most English people react when I tell them that. My mother maintains that she wanted each and every one of us, but I think she just got a bit carried away after she was married. I suppose you're an only child? Only children are particularly appalled at the thought of sharing a house with lots of other brothers and sisters.'

'I'm...well, we're not really here to discuss my background, Miss McKee...'

It didn't escape her notice that he had reverted to a formal appellation now that he was no longer manipulating their conversation. 'Oh, it was merely a question. Are you an only child?'

'Well, yes, as a matter of fact, I am.'

'I thought so. Poor you. My mum always said that an only child is a lonely child. Were you lonely as a child?'

'This is a ridiculous digression,' Kane muttered darkly. 'We were talking about your living arrangements.'

'So we were,' Shannon agreed readily. She took a small sip from her coffee, enjoying the sensation of sitting and having someone else do the waiting for a change. Their cups had been refilled without her even noticing the intrusion.

'And your decision to leave Ireland and come down here?'

'I thought we'd already talked about that. I told you that I had references and that you could see them. My last company was very pleased with my performance, actually,' she continued.

'Did you leave because of Eric Gallway?'

The luminous green eyes cooled and she said steadily, 'That really is none of your business, Mr Lindley.'

'No, it isn't, is it?' he said softly, but his eyes implied otherwise. 'Now, there are one or two other minor considerations that come with this job,' he said slowly, resting both his elbows on the table and leaning towards her. He had rolled up the sleeves of his white shirt so that she had an ample view of strong forearms, liberally sprinkled with fine, dark hair.

'Minor considerations?' Shannon met his thoughtful, speculative look with a stirring of unease. What minor considerations? She didn't care for the word 'minor'. Somehow it brought to mind the word 'major'.

'There are a few duties connected with this job that will require some overtime...'

She breathed a sigh of relief. She wasn't afraid of hard work and clock-watching had never been one of her problems. If anything, she'd often found herself staying on to work when she could have been going home.

'I'm fine with overtime, Mr Lindley,' she said quickly. 'Alfredo will vouch for that.'

'Good, good.' He paused and his dark eyes flitted across her face. 'These duties, however, are possibly not quite what you have in mind.'

'What do they involve, Mr Lindley?' Shannon asked faintly, for once lost for words in the face of the myriad possibilities filling her imaginative mind. She hoped that he wasn't about to spring some illegal suggestion on her because she'd just become accustomed to thinking that gainful employment was within her reach and to have it summarily snatched away would be almost more of a blow than the original loss of her job.

'I have a child, Miss McKee...'

'You *have a child*?'

'These things *do* happen as an outcome of sexual intercourse when no contraception has been used,' Kane said with overdone patience. 'As,' he added mildly, 'you are probably aware.'

Shannon failed to take offence at his tone. 'I—simply never associated you with a child,' she stammered, realising belatedly that her admission might give him the idea that she had been speculating wildly about him behind his back.

'And may I ask why?'

'You just don't look...the fatherly sort...' She shrugged helplessly. 'I mean,' she said hurriedly, as his eyebrows slanted upwards, 'you were always at the restaurant so early... I just assumed that you weren't much of a family man... How old is your child?'

'Eight and it's a she. Her name's Eleanor.'

'Oh, right.' Shannon paused long enough to digest this piece of information. 'And if you don't mind me asking, what does all this have to do with me?'

'At the moment I have a nanny in place to—'

'You have *a nanny in place*?' She gave a snort of derisory laughter.

'Would you do me the favour of not interrupting me every five seconds?'

'Sorry. It's just the expression you used.'

'I have a nanny in place who takes Eleanor to school in the mornings and brings her back home. Under normal circumstances, I would have a live-in nanny but Carrie has always insisted on having the evenings to herself and I've been loath to replace her because she's been there since Eleanor was a baby.'

'What about your wife? Does she work long hours as well?' Shannon's voice was laced with curiosity.

'My wife is dead.' He glanced down and she felt a rush of compassion for him and for his child. She tried to imagine a life with no siblings, no mother, an absent father and a nanny—and failed.

'I'm sorry.' She paused and then asked curiously, 'When did she die?'

'When Eleanor was born, actually.' There was a dead flatness in his voice which she recognised. She'd heard her mother use that tone whenever someone asked her about her husband. She'd used detachment to forestall questions she didn't want to answer. 'The pregnancy was fraught, although the birth was relatively simple. Three hours after Eleanor was born, my wife haemorrhaged to death.'

'I'm so very sorry, Mr Lindley.'

'So occasionally I might need you to act as babysitter, for want of a better word. My old secretary was very obliging in that respect but, as I said, she now lives in Dorset. Naturally, you would be paid handsomely for the inconvenience.'

Shannon cradled the cup in between her hands, rubbing the rim with her thumbs. 'Looking after a child could never be an inconvenience,' she said quietly.

'So.' He signalled for the bill and she could sense his eagerness to be off the subject of his child and back into the arena of discussing work. 'When would you be able to report for work?'

'Whenever you want.'

'What about next Monday morning? Eight-thirty

sharp. And, naturally, I needn't tell you that your first month will be a probationary one.'

'On both sides, Mr Lindley,' Shannon told him, just in case he got it into his head that she would somehow feel obliged to work for him even if she hated the job, simply because he had offered it to her out of duty.

'I wouldn't—' he graced her with such a powerful smile that her heart seemed to stop for a few seconds '—dream of expecting otherwise.' He stood up and politely offered her a lift to wherever she was going. When she declined, he nodded briefly in her direction before ushering her out of the coffee-bar.

The fresh, cold air whipped around her and for a few seconds, she had the unreal sensation that it had all been a vivid dream. She had always been particularly good at dreaming up improbable scenarios. Perhaps this was just another one. But, of course, it wasn't. She had quit one job and then Fate had smiled on her and decreed that she land another within hours of losing the first. Wasn't that just like life? Things, she had always thought, were never quite as black as they seemed. All you ever needed to do was leap over the first sticky patch and, sure enough, things would right themselves. There was always room for healthy optimism.

The healthy optimism stayed with Shannon for the remainder of the week and right into the weekend, which was spent with Sandy who seemed agog at the turn of events. She kept referring to 'the luck of the devil' and the way that Irish blarney could get a girl what she wanted until Shannon was forced to point out that the man was obviously impressed by all the secretarial potential he had spotted in her while she had waited tables.

'Ha! Perhaps he spotted *other potential*,' Sandy whispered darkly over their celebratory pizza.

But even that failed to quench her optimism.

She dressed very carefully on the Monday morning, making sure that everything matched and that there were no unknowing eccentric touches which had always been permissible at the radio station and at Alfredo's but most certainly would not be in most normal working environments. She looked regretfully at her floppy hat as she left the bedsit, and at her flat black lace-up shoes which were her faithful companions whether accompanied by skirt or trousers. Neither would do. Blue skirt, white blouse, blue and black checked jacket, which unfortunately was the only one she possessed and as a hand-me-down from one of her sisters didn't fit quite right, and, of course, her coat, one of her more expensive purchases from her working life at the radio station.

Her hair had presented a bit of a problem. Braids didn't seem right for a secretarial job in a normal office environment, but wearing it loose wasn't an option because as far as she was concerned, it was just too *red*, too *beacon-like*, so she tied it into a low ponytail which she held in place with a large, tortoiseshell barrette.

Shannon decided, as she caught the underground to the address Kane Lindley had written down for her, that her mother would have loved her outfit but her brothers and sisters would have fallen over laughing. Although she wasn't the youngest in the family, she was the last girl and so her elder sisters had mothered her. She was the only one in the family with red hair and somehow the red hair had always made her look much younger than her years. Thank heavens she had tied it back. Severely. She was about to embark on a severe career path, she decided, working for a man who would certainly not tolerate too much gaiety within the four walls of his office.

Her first taste of exactly how different her job would be compared to the last two was when she arrived at the office which turned out to be in a building all smoked glass and, as she entered, marble floors and plants in the foyer. Mr Lindley, she was told by the receptionist who was separated from the public by a large, smooth circular desk, was waiting for her and that if she took the lift to the fourth floor, she would be directed to his office.

By the time Shannon was standing outside his door, she was fast losing faith in her office skills. They had certainly done nicely in her previous two jobs, but did radio stations and restaurants really lend themselves to the sort of top-class working skills needed in a place like this? Somewhere with thick carpets and enclosed offices and people hurrying like ants from computer terminals to fax machines and photocopiers? Her carefully thought-out clothes seemed hideously informal next to the smartly dressed women she had spied, who seemed to be in a uniform of grey suits and black pumps.

She tentatively knocked at the door, which was opened by a middle-aged woman with iron grey hair and sharp eyes.

'I'm sorry,' Shannon stammered. 'Actually, I'm looking for Mr Lindley's office. The girl at Reception—'

'Should have called me to come and fetch you,' the woman said, interrupting her nervous explanation. 'I shall have to have a word with her. Step inside, Miss McKee. Allow me first of all to introduce myself. I'm Sheila Goddard. I don't normally work for Mr Lindley, although it has to be said that he hasn't found a suitable replacement for his previous secretary for...well, frankly, months, and I've spent quite a bit of my time covering. Most inconvenient.' She gave Shannon a look that seemed to imply that this inconvenience was somehow her fault.

'This will be your office. As you can see, Mr Lindley's office is just beyond the inner door. Now, my dear, I must confess that we were all a little surprised when Mr Lindley informed us that he had found himself a permanent secretary...'

Not as surprised as I was to be offered the job, she thought. 'I'm on one month's probation,' Shannon pointed out quickly, as she looked around the large outer office with its walnut desk and swivel chair and discreet company advertising pictures framed on the walls. Her optimism was fading fast in the face of all this sterile, hygienic space. No one around, no one to occasionally chat to. She might very well go mad within the month.

'Naturally,' Sheila said. 'You may join the line of unsuitable candidates, which is why I did suggest to Mr Lindley that it might have been a bit *rash* to take you on full time rather than as a temporary.'

'If you don't mind me asking, why exactly has there been a long line of unsuitable candidates?'

'Mr Lindley,' Sheila said ominously, 'is a demanding boss. Anything less than first rate never satisfies him.' She knocked respectfully at the imposing door separating the two offices, giving Shannon ample time to accommodate the prospect of trying to work for a monster who would attack at the first sign of a typing error.

The monster, waiting for her behind his desk, was on the telephone when she entered and he carried on talking, his voice clipped, while Shannon looked all around her, taking in the even more sterile surroundings of his office, unbroken by any hint of personality. Not even a picture or two of his daughter in sight. When there was nothing else to look at without doing damage to her neck muscles, she finally rested her green eyes on him. As he spoke, he leaned back in the leather chair, nodding at whatever was being said, answering solely in monosyllables.

'Right,' he said, as soon as he had replaced the receiver. 'You're here.'

'With my references,' Shannon agreed. 'But I must be honest, Mr Lindley, you were very kind to employ me but I don't think this arrangement is going to work out.' She pushed the references over to him and he began scanning them, then he sat back and looked at her.

'Why not?'

'Because this isn't the sort of working environment I'm used to at all. I really don't think I'll be suitable for the position.'

'Why don't you let me be the one to decide? Would you like some coffee? Tea? While I explain what your specific duties will involve?'

'No, thank you.'

'You're nervous.' He sat back and looked at her with his hands loosely folded on his lap. 'I'd never thought it of you, reds.'

'I'm not nervous.' Pointless, she thought, trying to tell him to use her full surname. 'It's just that…this is all a bit too formal for me… I wouldn't want to waste your time.'

'Very considerate of you,' he said drily. 'Your references are excellent. You're computer literate, you're willing to accept responsibilities… What makes you think you'd be wasting my time?'

'Apparently you've run through quite a number of unsatisfactory secretaries. Well, either the recruitment agencies have all been failing to do their jobs, or else you're a difficult man to work for.'

'I set high standards, if that's what you mean. Now, stop wittering about letting me down and let's start getting down to business. When I'm finished going through one or two clients with you and explaining what we do here, you can trot off to Personnel and sign your contract of employment.' He stood up, and glanced down at his watch, flicking back the cuff of his sleeve to expose dark hair gently curling at the strap.

'I have meetings this afternoon, but I shall leave you to do the basics. Some letters, faxes, e-mails. You can fence incoming calls by taking messages and I'll get back to them later. Sheila's always down the corridor if you run into difficulties.' He could see doubt stamped in her wary green eyes and he wondered, in passing, whether she realised exactly how appealing it made her.

'Look, if you really don't want to work for the company, I won't force you to stay. I can't force you to stay. The door's there and you're more than welcome to walk right through it and keep on walking until you get to an agency that has vacancies for interesting jobs in exciting, informal environments. Clearly you think that all this is just a little too stuffy for you. Perhaps you think that bosses should just lounge around all day in garish clothes with their feet on the desk, making as few demands as possible on their staff so as not to interrupt the enjoyment of it all. But,' he said, 'I can guarantee that your pay will be more than double what you were earning at that restaurant. And that's excluding what you'll personally be paid by me for anything you do involving my daughter.'

Shannon gave him a wry look to match his own. 'I'll give it a go. I'm as open to bribery as the next person.' Their eyes tangled in perfect mutual and amused understanding before she looked away.

She preceded her new boss into her office and sat down at the desk. He watched as her skirt rode a few centimetres higher, exposing slim, pale thighs through her tights. She'd disposed of the coat and the peculiar jacket, revealing a blouse that fitted snugly over her small breasts.

'Clients.' Kane Lindley cleared his throat and frowned in concentration as she flicked on the computer and waited for him to pick up the sentence. 'Accounts. Yes. Well, you'll be expected to update accounts and everything has to be filed in alphabetical order.' He leaned forward so that his forearm rested on the desk, almost brushing her bare skin.

'A lot of business is conducted overseas, so it would be helpful if you knew the money markets. Not in any great detail, but it would give you some idea of what is likely to be profitable and what is not. Now the media group I've just taken over…' He leant past her to flick back to the main menu so that he could begin running through details of the finances of the various companies under the one umbrella and as he did so she felt him brush against her breast. She drew away, a little shaken at the fleeting contact.

'Generally speaking, you won't be needed to accompany me to meetings.' He moved away from the desk and chose instead to pull up a chair so that his eyes could remain safely fixed on the same level as hers. 'However, you *will* need to check every e-mail I get when I'm not in the office and I get quite a number. In time, you should be able to deal with a good proportion of those.'

Shannon, turning to look at him, was a little disconcerted to find him quite so close to her. Close enough for her to distinguish the various shades of dark brown and black in his eyes and to breathe in the musky scent of male body, unimpeded by any colognes.

'Now,' he said finally, sitting back and pushing himself away from the desk, 'any questions?'

Shannon swivelled her chair to face him. 'About work?'

He looked at her wryly. 'No. I thought we might just have a general discussion about world affairs.'

'Don't you get a little lonely stuck out in this office on your own?'

'*Lonely?* Don't I get *a little lonely*?'

'Yes. You know...surely you don't spend the entire day focused on work. You must need to chat now and again...'

'*Chat?*'

'To people? Maybe when you break off to have a cup of coffee?'

'When I break off to have a cup of coffee, reds, I actually normally remain at my desk and more often than not I devote my attention to paperwork while I'm having it,' he said crushingly, and she nodded.

'Then how do you know what's going on in your company? You know, if you don't get around and hear the gossip on the ground floor?'

'*Hear the gossip?*'

'Well, you *did* ask me whether I had any questions,' Shannon trailed off, when he continued to stare at her as though she were crazy. 'As far as the actual *work* goes, I think I can handle it. I might be a bit slow to start with, of course. Until I find my feet.'

'I shouldn't think it'll take you very long,' he said. 'I've told Linda in Personnel to expect you some time before lunch.' With a swift, graceful movement, he stood up and eyed her blandly. 'Right now I shall be busy with meetings, so I probably won't see you until tomorrow. Linda will fill you in on all of this, but if you're interested, there's an office restaurant on the ground floor. I suspect that's where all the chat and gossip occurs.'

'Perhaps *you* should eat there more often in that case,' Shannon said with a slow grin.

'Actually,' he threw at her over his shoulder, as he slipped on his jacket and adjusted his tie, 'I do. Whenever I get the chance.'

He walked towards the door, then paused before turning to look at her. 'I think it might be a good idea if you met Eleanor. Carrie's been staying on late to accommodate me over the past two months, but now that you're here we can work something out so that she can get back to her social life.'

'I thought the babysitting arrangement was more on an…occasional basis,' Shannon faltered. 'And what about *my* social life?'

'Oh.' He walked slowly towards her, rubbing his chin with his hand as though startled at the concept of her having a social life. 'I thought you had come to London to nurse a broken heart. Don't you spend all your free time pining?'

Shannon flushed at his blatant and cheerful disregard for boundaries. 'Actually, if you read any self-help book, you'll discover that women with broken hearts immediately rush off to cultivate new and exciting social lives,' she replied tartly. She wondered whether dinner dates with Sandy constituted a new and exciting social life. Having come to London, she had quickly realised that the novel taste of freedom from her brothers and sisters and extended family members also carried a downside. Namely, that there was no handy cushion to protect her from her nights spent on her own. She went out with Sandy and with some of the other staff who worked at Alfredo's and was gradually building up a social life of sorts, but it was hardly humming.

'Well,' Kane conceded, 'I normally return home by eight, so your exciting social life shouldn't suffer too much.'

'By *eight*? When do you ever get to see your daughter?'

'I usually try and keep weekends free,' he muttered, turning away as a dark flush spread up his neck. 'Do you know your way around London?' He bent over and scribbled his address on a piece of paper. 'No, forget that. I'll get my driver to come and collect you, say, Friday evening? Around seven-thirty? Eleanor usually stays up late on a Friday as there's no school on a Saturday.'

'I'm sure I can find my way to your house, Mr Lindley.' She looked at the address and wondered how far it would be from an underground station. She wasn't averse to walking but walking at night, freezing cold and potentially without any real clue as to where she was heading, wasn't her idea of fun.

'I wouldn't dream of it.' He smiled briefly. 'After all, you're the one who will be doing me the service.'

'What is she like?' Shannon asked curiously, folding the piece of paper and stuffing it into her bag.

'Small, blonde hair, blue eyes.'

'Actually, I meant her personality.'

'Oh, Eleanor is...very quiet.' He frowned and seemed to be thinking of some other way he could find of describing her. 'Doesn't give any trouble at all.'

To Shannon, that hardly sounded like a great description of an eight-year-old child. I mean, she thought, if you can't get into a spot of trouble when you're eight, then when on earth *can* you? She had spent most of her formative years getting into trouble! When she'd left school at sixteen, she could remember the headmistress telling her mother that never in the history of the school had one parent paid so many visits.

'Right,' Shannon said in a subdued, reflective voice.

'Don't forget, if you run into anything you can't handle, and I'm not around, Sheila will help you out. She knows as much about this business as I do, probably.' He moved towards the door and stopped to say with a gravity in his voice that was only belied by the glint in his eye, 'And don't forget the office canteen. It's a hotbed of gossip and intrigue. Let me know if you hear about any insurrections I should beware of.'

She could have sworn she heard a chuckle as Kane shut the door behind him and she was left with the computer, a stack of letters to type and the prospect of dinner *en famille* in four days' time with a man who was reluctantly beginning to intrigue her even more than he had when she'd been serving him his coffee and bagels.

CHAPTER THREE

KANE LINDLEY'S house was as far removed from Shannon's expectations as it was possible to be.

She'd expected something modern and austere, perhaps a penthouse suite in a renovated building with thick white carpets to drown out the noise of an eight-year-old child, whom she imagined wandering forlornly amid the luxury, searching for places to hide from a largely absent father.

But when the chauffeur-driven car turned into a pair of wrought-iron gates, the house confronting her was an ivy-clad Victorian house with neatly trimmed lawns. The outside lights revealed mature trees shading some swings and a slide.

She rang the doorbell, feeling her stomach muscles tense. Kane Lindley was proving to be a very good boss, so how was it that she still felt a little quiver of alarm every time she saw him? In fact, even when he was working in his office and out of sight, there was still a part of her that seemed tuned in to his presence, waiting for him to emerge. She assumed that it was all wrapped up in the usual nervousness of being new to a job.

She might have surmounted this initial nervousness if he'd been out of the office much, as he'd implied he would be at their first interview, but, in fact, he was in a great deal. Through the partially open door, she was always aware of his clipped voice as he conversed on the phone or else his steady silence as he worked through paperwork and on his computer. Ever so often he would call her in and dictate something, and then he would swivel his chair away from his desk and talk fluently and smoothly at her, frowning as he spoke, while his fingers lightly drummed his thigh. And he never failed to peer in at least twice a day just to see how she was progressing.

She couldn't really see why he hadn't been able to find a suitable secretary. It was hardly as if he was prone to dramatic mood swings or unpleasantly critical behaviour, and she could only think that his pace was maybe too fast for someone with too little experience. If nothing else, working at Alfredo's and at the radio station had promoted a healthy ability to think quickly and react without confusion to abrupt changes of routine.

A rotund, middle-aged woman answered the door, introduced herself as Mrs Porter and informed Shannon, without preamble, that Kane was waiting for her in the sitting room.

'And where's Eleanor?' Shannon asked, anxious to make sure that the object of this evening visit hadn't done something unfortunate, like gone to bed. A cosy little dinner with only Kane Lindley for company, while his daughter innocently slumbered upstairs, wasn't an appealing prospect. But Eleanor, she was told, was in the sitting room with her father and was, she was also told in a confidential whisper, eagerly looking forward to meeting Shannon.

'If you ask me,' Mrs Porter said, her voice sinking lower so that Shannon had to strain to hear what she was saying, 'Mr Lindley should have remarried a long time ago. A child needs a mother figure. No stability, that's her problem, poor little mite. Young Carrie is fine with her, but she really needs someone permanent. Not these women friends who seem to drop in one minute and out the next.'

Shannon nodded, loath to continue talking in this manner about someone else's private life yet avidly curious to find out more about Kane. Women friends? He had women friends? Of course he had, she thought, wildly trying to imagine what this long line of inappropriate women friends was like. He always seemed so controlled that the idea of him flinging himself passionately at a woman, growing weak at the knees whenever she came into the room, was beyond the powers of even *her* imagination.

Fortunately, the temptation to elicit more information on this suddenly raunchy side of Kane Lindley was abruptly halted by Mrs Porter pushing open the door to the sitting room and then stepping aside so that Shannon could enter.

'I'll be off now, Mr Lindley, if that's all right with you. The food will just need heating up, but the table's all set.'

'Heating up?'

'I can help, Dad.' There was a childish eagerness to Eleanor's voice that made Shannon ache.

'Eleanor, this is Shannon, my new secretary. You're going to be seeing a bit of her when I'm not around.'

'Hello.' She smiled briefly, then turned to her father with a pleading face. 'But, really, Dad, I can help. I know what to do. Honestly.'

'Eleanor, darling, you're far too young to be doing anything in the kitchen. Most domestic accidents originate in the kitchen, did you know that? There are knives, fire, pans of boiling water—'

'She can do a bit, Mr Lindley,' Shannon interrupted, growing impatient with his listing of danger points which made the average kitchen sound like a death trap. 'When I was Eleanor's age, I was already doing a few basic things.' She sneaked a glance at Eleanor who was gaping at her with shy gratitude. 'You just have to make sure that there's supervision and—'

'*You* may have been preparing three-course meals at the age of eight, but Eleanor didn't have your sturdy upbringing.' He turned to his daughter. 'Shannon comes from a family of seven children.'

'*Seven?* Wow!' The revelation had turned her eyes into saucers. 'How lucky! I wish…' Her voice trailed off and her eyes flitted across to her father.

'I'll make sure I supervise her, Mr Lindley,' Shannon said hurriedly, before the telling sentence could be completed. 'I mean, Eleanor, don't you do home economics at school? A bit of baking and stuff?'

'Not really,' Eleanor admitted, frowning.

'There, you see! Even the school realises the limits of letting children loose with dangerous objects.' His eyebrows rose with the satisfaction of someone who has proved a point, and Shannon flushed hotly.

'Actually, Mr Lindley—'

'Kane. It's ridiculous for us to be on such formal terms. And I can see from the indignant expression on your face that I'm about to be subjected to a lecture on the importance of teaching young children how to play with fire.'

'I wouldn't dream of lecturing you on anything of the sort,' Shannon informed him in a huffy voice, 'but what I'm talking about here is a wooden spoon, a bowl and a bit of stirring perhaps. How many young children do you personally know who have fallen victim to a sharp cut from a wooden spoon? And how many serious domestic accidents have been caused from a bit of stirring?'

'We do woodwork at school,' Eleanor interrupted helpfully. 'Don't we, Dad? Do you remember that box I made for you a few months ago? The one with the lid that could open and close?'

'Yes, of course I do.' But Shannon could tell from the vague expression on his face that the last thing currently stored in his memory bank was a box with a lid that could open and close.

'I hate to criticise you,' Shannon muttered as they walked towards the kitchen with Eleanor eagerly leading the way like a proud, albeit diminutive, hostess, 'but do you take any interest in what your daughter does at school?'

'And I hate to criticise *you*, reds' he muttered back, 'but I hope you're not going to launch into a load of psychobabble about workaholic fathers.'

'So you admit you're a workaholic.'

'I don't admit anything of the sort,' he said, *sotto voce*. 'And just in case the ground rules of this contract have escaped you, you're employed to look after Eleanor for a few hours a day after you leave work, not to analyse me.'

'Smells wonderful in here,' Shannon exclaimed, ignoring his remark.

'Mrs Porter always does the cooking when Dad entertains his women friends at home,' Eleanor said. 'I laid the table. I wasn't too sure where the soup spoons went, so I thought I'd just stick them in the bowls.'

'Excellent!' Kane said heartily, avoiding eye contact with Shannon. He moved over to the stove and flicked on the fire, looking dubiously inside the saucepan as though not too sure what his next move should be.

'I think you're meant to pour it into the bowls,' Shannon said, and Eleanor gave a stifled giggle. 'Surely, with all those women friends you've been entertaining, you must have got to grips with the basic food-serving procedure.'

'Oh, Mrs Porter usually does all that,' Eleanor informed her earnestly. 'Doesn't she, Dad? She had to leave tonight because her son is poorly. He's twelve years old and he twisted his ankle in a game of rugby at school.'

'A dangerous sport. I'm surprised schools allow it,' Shannon said piously. 'On the whole, I'd say it was a darn sight more dangerous than home economics, actually.'

'Or woodwork, even,' Eleanor replied, tucking into her soup and licking her lips after every mouthful. 'Last week, Claire Thompson hurt her finger when her bowl dropped on her hand.'

Shannon made tutting noises under her breath. The soup was delicious. No wonder he used Mrs Porter whenever he entertained at home. All those hundreds of women who probably flitted in and out of his life like ships in the night. Did they know, she wondered, when they started dating Kane that they would end up as a ship in the night?

'And I can remember getting a paper cut once at school,' Shannon mused in the startled voice of someone putting two and two together and suddenly arriving at the correct answer. 'Perhaps schools should ban paper.'

Eleanor started to laugh. 'Or food at lunchtime, in case someone spills some over themselves and gets burnt!'

'Or desks! A child can get a nasty bang on the edge of a desk if she's not careful!'

'Oh, shut up, the two of you,' Kane said, smiling at his daughter. Her face was flushed. 'And you can start on your home economics course,' he added, wiping his mouth with his napkin and sitting back in the chair, 'by clearing away these bowls to the sink.'

By the end of the meal, Eleanor was becoming more what Shannon envisaged an eight-year-old child should be like. Her voice was less of a whisper and she was laughing as she related things that had happened at school, what people had said, what games they played at break.

'When are you going to be coming to stay with me?' she asked Shannon, pausing on her way out of the room to hear the answer.

When Shannon looked enquiringly at Kane, he said, raising his hands in mock surrender, 'I'll be a bit late home next Monday. Can you make it then after work? Carrie will collect Eleanor from school as usual and then she'll leave when you get here to replace her.'

So that was settled. It was only when Eleanor had been escorted upstairs by her father, and Shannon was left alone in the stillness of the kitchen, that she felt a sneaking suspicion that she had somehow been manipulated. She also had the uneasy feeling that she was being drawn into a family unit which would somehow undermine her bid for freedom.

Part of her mission in coming all the way to London, aside from the obvious reason of physically distancing herself from Ireland and its nagging, unpleasant memories, had been to try her feet at walking without the aid of her family around her. So what was she doing? Getting involved with another family.

'She likes you.' Kane's voice snapped her out of her worrying speculation and Shannon turned to him with a bright smile. 'Some coffee in the sitting room?' He moved over to the kettle and switched it on.

'I really should be heading back, actually.'

'At nine-thirty? On a Friday night? We need to talk about how often you're prepared to take over from Carrie,' he told her bluntly. 'Eleanor...' He perched against the kitchen counter and folded his arms thoughtfully. 'To be honest, I've never seen Eleanor respond so quickly to anyone.'

Shannon had a sharp mental picture of Eleanor in the presence of the mysterious line of women, which had been preying on her mind more than she was willing to admit, shyly retiring, insecure, mouse-like, seeking her father's approval even though the furthest thing from his mind would have been the attention-seeking of his daughter.

'I always knew that having so many brothers and sisters would come in handy some day.' She followed him into the sitting room and sat in the deep chair closest to the fire, curling her legs underneath her like a cat.

'Shall we scrap the coffee and have a nightcap instead?' Kane moved over to a wooden cabinet in the corner of the room and clicked open a concealed door to reveal a healthy supply of glasses and drinks. 'What would you like? I have pretty much everything. What about a brandy? Or a glass of port?'

'I'll have a port,' Shannon told him. 'You have a lovely house, Mr Lindley...Kane. How long have you lived here?'

'My wife and I bought this house when we were first married...'

'And you stayed on after...?'

'After she died?' He strolled over to her and handed her a glass of red liquid, his fingers brushing hers as she took it from him. Then he sat on the sofa and crossed his legs, resting his hand lightly on his knee. 'I thought about moving, but only briefly. I like the house and, at any rate, you can't run away from your memories. They'll follow you to the end of the earth. You just have to learn to cope with them. Now, what did you think about Eleanor? It's not an ideal situation, leaving work to come immediately here, and I expect you to be honest and tell me now if you don't think you'll be able to do it on a regular basis.'

Shannon took a sip of port and it rushed down her throat like fire. 'By regular basis, you mean...?'

'Every day after work,' he said lazily, 'but, of course, that's open to negotiation.'

'Don't you get back early *any* evening?' Another sip of port. This time the fire seemed slightly less potent, although her head was now beginning to feel fuzzy. Her new-found freedom and aspirations towards a exciting, cosmopolitan lifestyle hadn't included nurturing a taste for alcohol. She still only drank wine, and in small amounts, and the port was like a bullet being fired into her brain.

'Some evenings. And I always make sure that I keep the weekends free.'

'Hmm. That's big of you.' She could grow to quite like this drink, she thought, swigging back the remainder in the glass and making a poor show of refusing a refill. Over dinner, with Eleanor present, Shannon had been a model of perfect behaviour. Aside from her brief debate on the relative safety of kitchen gadgets, she had chatted amiably to Eleanor about school and friends and hobbies, but after the glass of port she could feel the polite veneer beginning to slip a little.

That had always been her problem. She'd never been able to resist saying exactly what was on her mind, even though she'd had many an occasion to regret her lapses.

If she'd had ten pence for every time she'd spoken without thinking, according to her mother, she would have been a millionaire by her eighteenth birthday.

'I mean...' she said, deciding to go easy on the second glass of port. A little honesty was often bad enough but an overdose of it could be lethal. In fact, might lose her job, which she was already beginning to enjoy, despite her initial reservations. 'You ask me about Eleanor...'

She frowned in the manner of someone focusing on a knotty problem when, in fact, she was simply struggling to gather her thoughts together so that she could formulate a sentence or two that made sense. 'I feel a little sorry for her, to be honest. She's so desperate to get some of your attention.'

'Desperate to get my attention? She has my attention whenever I'm around! And whatever she wants, she gets.'

'Have you noticed that every time she says anything, she looks to you for approval? It's as though...' As though *what*? Time, she thought, for another sip of the yummy burgundy liquid that was really very helpful when it came to clarifying her thought processes. 'As though...she doesn't want to put a foot wrong in case she disappoints you!'

'How on earth could Eleanor disappoint me?' He shot her a wry look and said mildly, 'Are you sure your observations aren't originating from two glasses of port?'

'Of course not!' Shannon laughed merrily. 'Actually, I've always been able to hold my drink! You asked me about what I thought of your daughter, and I told you. In my opinion...' she leaned forward and grasped the collar of her coffee-coloured blouse which was, she had thought earlier, the perfect outfit for a prospective child-minder—babysitter meeting her charge but was now revealing an offputting tendency to gape and expose the lacy top of her matching beige coloured bra… 'Shannon needs a mother.'

'Oh, that's your opinion, is it?'

Why did she get the impression that Kane was humouring her?

'Yes, as a matter of fact, it is. Girls need mothers, it's as simple as that.'

He appeared to give this statement a bit of thought. Then he said in an infuriatingly amused voice, 'Well, at the risk of disappointing you, there's no mother substitute in the picture at the moment.'

'Not even from the long line of women who flit in and out of your life?'

'Ah. I wondered when you would bring that up. I caught that expressive little flicker in your eyes when Eleanor was talking about Mrs Porter and her handy knack of whipping up meals for all these women who come and go.' He settled back comfortably on the sofa and linked his fingers behind his dark head while his eyes continued to survey her face with lazy amusement. 'Now, Shannon, tell me truthfully, do I look like the kind of man who has a queue of women lining up to go out with him? Hmm?'

That compelled her to look at him. Out of his impeccably tailored office suit, he looked less conservative, but only slightly less so. His khaki-coloured trousers and green short sleeved shirt and brown loafers were all traditional garb. His black hair was raked back from his face and there was no stubble to suggest anything wickedly decadent about the man sitting in front of her.

'Out of the mouths of babes…' she said weakly.

'You haven't answered my question.'

'All right. Then the answer is yes!'

'Because I'm exciting and sexy?' he asked drily, enjoying the flush that was creeping steadily up her cheeks and the nervous fluttering of her fingers as she slipped them around the stem of the glass and drained the remainder of her port.

'Because,' Shannon said, 'Eleanor would have no reason to lie. Anyway,' she said defiantly, 'perhaps you're too fussy when it comes to women. Surely you've felt the need to remarry, settle down, perhaps have more children…?'

'I haven't found the right woman. I told you, I'm a sad old man who will probably end up on my own with no one to look after me but my faithful housekeeper who knows how to cook five-star meals.'

He grinned boyishly at Shannon and she went a little pinker. She suspected that if she felt round the edge of her bra, she would find a thin layer of nervous perspiration. For a man who never raised his voice, at least not at work, ever, he still had the ability to make most people feel flustered. It was something to do with the laser-like sharpness of his eyes. Right now her port-clogged mind was feeling very flustered indeed.

'But still you keep trying.'

'As you must.' The smile was still playing at the corners of his mouth as if her unwarranted intrusive line of questioning was a source of enjoyment rather than discomfort. 'How else will I ever find Mrs Right?' he asked in a sanctimonious voice.

'Is there any specific routine I should stick to with Eleanor?' Shannon asked, reflecting weakly that her crisp tone of voice was a little late in coming. It also wouldn't last very long, not with two glasses of port swimming around inside her. She tilted her head to one side to lend more authority to her tone and felt a little giddy in the process.

'I believe Carrie makes sure that homework is done, food eaten, bath taken and some reading done before bed. Sometimes I make it home by book-reading time but, as you've seen for yourself, it's impossible to stick to any kind of timetable in my line of work.'

'And would you prefer it if you could?' Shannon asked curiously.

'Of course,' he answered, not that she believed a word of that. She doubted whether Kane Lindley ever consulted his watch when it came to leaving work behind. Well, as his secretary, she could very well arrange a more sociable timetable for him when it came to seeing his daughter more regularly. In fact, she decided that she would make it a top priority.

'So, how are you finding the job so far? As invigorating as the restaurant business?'

'More concentrated, if anything,' she admitted. 'Alfredo never had much of a conscience when it came to relieving me from secretarial duties when there was a shortage of waiters. He said that it was the typically Italian way of running things.' She grinned. 'Actually, he had a reliable habit of blaming most things on his Italian temperament. I think he expected us to fall in line because his temperament, according to him, was volatile but basically non-negotiable.'

'And you never questioned that?'

'I'm accustomed to volatile people!'

'And aside from the temperamental Italian, we poor Londoners must seem very tame in comparison.'

Shannon was unsure how to deal with this informal, teasing question. Within the confines of the office, Kane was formal and utterly self-controlled. She had seen how he dealt with other members of staff. Polite, courteous, the epitome of the professional man, not given to chit-chat. She realised that in accepting the job of babysitting his daughter during the week, she had opened a door to a less predictable side of him. Less predictable and more disconcerting.

'Have you made any friends in the company yet?' he asked, relieving her of the task of answering his unanswerable question, even though she would have been more relieved if he'd ended all conversation by standing up, yawning and saying goodnight. 'I've more or less left you to your own devices. What have you been doing at lunchtimes?'

'The canteen, actually. Sheila felt sorry for me and took me down on my first day and introduced me to some of the people who work in the other departments. In fact, did you know that there's something called the Lottery Club?'

'The Lottery Club?' He looked at her with a bewildered expression.

'Yes!' She leaned forward, pressing her hands against the sides of the sofa, and stared earnestly at him. Or, at least, she hoped that her stare was earnest. If a little unsteady at the edges. 'Apparently lots of people are on it. They all put in money to do the lottery and then on a Friday they go down to the pub to celebrate the fact that they probably haven't won! In fact, I would have been there now if I hadn't been, well…here instead. But next Friday they're all going to a club in Leicester Square and I've been invited to go along. It'll be fun!'

In fact, she couldn't wait. This was what she had come to London for, she decided. Fun with a capital F! Despite her exuberant personality, she was more of a homebody than she would have ever cared to admit to anyone, and she had eschewed clubbing in Ireland for the more mundane activities of going to the movies with her friends or having a meal out at the local pizza place or Chinese restaurant. The first she'd tasted of a more glitzy lifestyle had been during her brief and traumatic fling with Eric Gallway, and even then, she thought sourly, she'd been more interested in running around behind him like a pet pooch than enjoying the nightclubs he had taken her to. It had been one of his many angry criticisms of her when the whole thing had blown up. That she was boring and unsophisticated. That she was like a teenager, but without the sense of daring.

Daring was something she was currently striving for, and next week's fun at a club would be the first step.

Unfortunately, Kane was looking at her with a concerned expression, as though she had inadvertently informed him that she intended to become a lap dancer for the evening. Perhaps, she thought crossly, he was wondering whether she was a suitable candidate after all to look after his child for a handful of hours every week. Perhaps, on top of the children-should-be-allowed-in-the-kitchen attitude, an admission of wanting to go to a nightclub in Leicester Square was confirmation of her juvenile tendencies.

'Sounds like a bundle of laughs,' he said drily. 'Even though you don't look too convinced.'

'I happen to be very convinced,' Shannon informed him, tilting her chin up.

'And you've been to clubs before, have you?'

'Of course I've been to clubs! Dublin is very well stocked with them, in case you didn't know. And what makes you think that I haven't been to any? I may not be a Londoner born and bred, but I'm not exactly green round the ears!'

'I do apologise if I've given you the impression that that's what I thought,' he said, in an unapologetic voice, 'but for some reason I got the impression that you were a family person, perhaps even rather sheltered.'

'I used to be,' she corrected him firmly, breaking off to ask for a top-up, just to prove that wild and daring was the woman she was and not young and uninitiated, which had been Eric's opinion of her. Young, uninitiated and therefore ready for a little corruption. 'But we all grow up, don't we?' Her head was beginning to feel a little chaotic, and for some strange reason she had the maddest urge to shock him. He always looked so *unshockable*. If a mushroom cloud had gathered over his house and there had been a two-minute warning going off, she doubted whether he would have been galvanised into panicky action. She wondered madly what he would look like roused.

'And you've decided that now is your time to grow up.'

'I'm certainly looking for adventure,' she confided, leaning forward to retrieve her glass of port and recklessly not bothering to clasp the top of her blouse so that her small breasts could be tantalisingly glimpsed. No wonder he was pursued by women, she thought. They probably were all falling over themselves to rise to the challenge of making him lose control.

'Would this have anything to do with your experience in Ireland? Before you came down here?'

'What experience?' Shannon dodged, frankly glugging the port at this point.

'With Eric Gallway.' He stretched out his long legs in front of him, crossing them at the ankles, and proceeded to fix her with an unblinking stare.

'Nothing happened between Eric and me,' she muttered feebly.

'Which is why you threw hot food all over him.'

'Anyway,' she said with sullen resistance, 'as I've already told you, it's none of your business.'

'But in a way it is. The fact is, we're thinking of hiring him…'

'What? To work in your company?' Her stubborn expression was replaced with horror. She would pack in the job tomorrow if the alternative was running into Eric Gallway round every corner!

'Yes, as a matter of fact.'

'Then you can accept my resignation as of now.' She teetered to her feet, alarmed at how unsteady they felt, and hovered there, hoping that she could make it to the front door without losing either her dignity or, for that matter, her sense of balance.

'Oh, sit down! He won't be working where you are. He'll be working for my newly acquired media group, in front of the cameras. I gather the thought of that rather appealed to his vanity.'

Shannon sat back down. Sitting felt distinctly better.

'And the reason I want to know what happened between you is that I want you to tell me if there's any reason why we shouldn't hire the man.'

'Any reason like what?' She was beginning to feel vaguely cornered by this subtle battering of her defences.

'Oh, I don't know. Perhaps you uncovered something about him…'

'Oh, I uncovered something about him all right,' she said bitterly, 'but nothing that would make him unemployable.'

'And what was that?' His voice was a silky whisper and he leaned forward, resting his forearms on his thighs and staring intently at her. She sincerely wished he wouldn't do that. It made her feel giddy.

In the short, taut silence that followed his question, she could feel a reckless urge to confess everything to the man sitting in front of her. And why shouldn't she? It wasn't as though it were some dark, horrifying secret. In fact, it would be a relief to tell someone, someone unconnected with the whole affair. Since coming to London, she had maintained a rigid silence about the unfortunate episode, preferring to be accepted as the person she was now, and not judged in any way by what had happened in the past. But wasn't it more in keeping with the varnished exterior she was cultivating to laugh the whole incident off with a casual shrug and a knowing smile?

'I had an affair with him!' she confessed gaily, ruefully realising that her glass was once again empty just when she could have done with a bit of morale bolstering.

He nodded and failed to look nonplussed. 'How did you meet in the first place?'

'He came to the radio station to do an interview with my boss about the differences between working in Ireland as opposed to working in England. How things differed in the area of media and suchlike. Also our radio station was up and coming because it was small and really only dealt with local gossip.'

'And you fell for his charms, did you?' He stood up and watched patiently and expressionlessly while she wobbled to her feet, then he helpfully took her arm to steady her. 'I gather you're not accustomed to drink?'

He couldn't even be bothered to hear her out! He was too busy being paternalistic about the state of her intoxication! This was the Big City and confessions of affairs and broken hearts were a dime a dozen.

'Yes, I fell for him!' Shannon snapped, reluctantly grateful for the support of his arm because without it she had a sneaking feeling that she would plummet to the ground in an inelegant heap. 'He was a smooth talker. He took me places, promised me a future and then I found out that he was married!'

'Oh, dear,' he said sympathetically, as they made their way slowly towards the hall, where her coat was perched in the downstairs cloakroom. 'It must have come as quite a shock.'

'Married with two children!' Shock was a mild way of describing what she had felt at the revelation. She had felt the world collapse around her. 'And when I confronted him, he laughed! Said that I needed to grow up! Told me that married men had affairs all the time and that I would realise that if I wasn't too busy being a baby! He said that he was glad to be rid of me because I wouldn't…wouldn't…you know…'

'Wouldn't what?'

'Wouldn't sleep with him,' Shannon said. She felt a little tear of self-pity gather in the corner of her eye and she blinked several times, taking her time as she allowed him to slip her into her coat and telephone for his driver to come for her.

'He was a cad, reds,' Kane said gently, inclining her face to his with the pressure of a finger under her chin. 'He didn't deserve you. Forget him.'

'I have. I only brought up the subject because you asked.'

'Good girl.' He tapped her nose with the tip of his finger and smiled. Frankly, it was insulting. Next, he would say 'chin up' and tell her that she was only a kid after all.

'And I've seen the error of my ways,' she told him, all self-pity banished by sudden, swift anger at his response.

'Go for the good guy next time.' He nodded in a soothing way.

'Oh, just the opposite, actually,' she threw back at him. 'At my tender age, I've already discovered how men use women, so why not apply some of the same medicine to them? Starting,' she added, for further credibility, 'next Friday.'

CHAPTER FOUR

'AND...? How did your wild and exciting evening on Friday go? Was it everything you expected?'

Kane had finished briefing Shannon on what he wanted done and now he sat back in his leather chair and looked at her with a little smile. They had settled into a working routine that included a cup of coffee first thing in the morning in his office while he flicked through files, passing over what he wanted her to do, what meetings needed to be scheduled, what meetings needed to be cancelled and what clients needed to be contacted in order of priority. On the trip into work, she now found herself looking forward to that half-hour. In a strange way, it seemed to set her up for the rest of the day.

Shannon gathered up the files from the desk and rested them on her lap.

'It was scintillating,' she lied, casting her mind back to the pub where they had all met at eight for drinks, followed by a nightclub which had turned out to be a cramped dark space somewhere in Soho where the music had been too loud, the atmosphere too smoky and the crowd almost entirely composed of nineteen-year-old kids dressed in way-out clothes.

Having expected something a little more sophisticated, Shannon had settled at a table in the corner with three of the women from work and had spent the remainder of the evening comparing notes on how young the people had seemed to be and trying to identify the music which had not so much blared as throbbed with a steady bass beat that had been very good at promoting headaches. She'd had the odd dance with one of the guys from the company but there had been so many people on the dance floor that it had been difficult to move, never mind dance properly. By the time she had got back to her bedsit at one-thirty, her dress and tights had smelled of cigarette smoke and had born the telltale patchy spots of spilled drinks.

'Scintillating... Where did you go?'

She gave him the name of the club, safe in the knowledge that the last place Kane Lindley would have heard of would have been a nightclub for wild, young things—most of whom hadn't looked old enough to earn a living, never mind be in possession of the money needed to have a good time for hours in a nightclub in central London.

'You went *there*!' He sounded horrified and she felt her hackles rise at the tone of his voice. Now, more than ever, she was determined to drive home to him what an exciting evening it had been. 'I don't suppose you realised that that place has a reputation for illicit drugs? Not exactly fertile ground for meeting new people. Well, not unless you're interested in meeting boys who probably haven't started shaving yet! What would your mother say?'

'My mother isn't here!' Shannon declared icily, 'so she isn't going to say anything, is she? And,' she continued, fixing him with a gimlet stare, 'how do you know about this place? Don't tell me you go there on a weekend to live it up!'

'Why not? Can't you picture me slugging back pints of lager and gyrating on a dance floor with eighteen-year-old girls?'

Actually, Shannon found it easier to picture herself growing five arms and three legs overnight. There was a quiet gallantry about Kane that resisted any notion of him misbehaving in any way in public. Or in private for that matter. She doubted if he had ever lost his self-control. He just wasn't that type of man.

'Frankly, no.' She rustled the files on her lap, waiting for his invisible signal that it was time for her to go, but he carried on looking at her, smiling.

'Maybe you're right,' he conceded in a low, amused voice. 'Eighteen-year-old girls don't interest me. And I can think of better ways of dancing than flinging myself around and bashing into everyone else.'

His voice left her in no doubt what form of dancing he had in mind and she felt faintly unsettled at the thought. She had a vision of him on a dance floor, his strong arms engulfing the woman with him, his body pressed erotically against hers, hips grinding against hips, face and hands buried into hair. Losing that iron self-control. His body trembling slightly in anticipation of what was to come. His voice thick with desire.

She gulped and shuffled the files a little harder.

Every so often a rogue thought would enter her head—that his innate gentlemanliness disguised something wild and dangerous, lurking suggestively beneath the surface.

'Can't you?' he prompted, and she looked at him with an addled expression.

'Can't I what?'

'Think of better ways of dancing?'

'Oh, yes,' Shannon said crisply. 'The foxtrot can be quite a laugh. And, of course, there's Irish dancing. You can't beat it for burning off calories.'

He gave a wry laugh and then said lightly, 'And I can

think of better ways of doing that as well. Eleanor,' he said, changing the subject before she could dwell on what he had said, 'seems to be quite taken with you. She tells me that you're fun. How are you finding it? Is the travelling too much of a hassle? It's dark by the time you leave and really I don't care to think of you traipsing through London on the underground to get back to your flat.'

'Oh, it's fine,' Shannon said airily, thinking of the dark, isolated walk once she left the underground and was heading back to her bedsit. The Victorian house which had been converted into bedsits was in a leafy, residential area but a residential area that only just managed to creep into the category of savoury. In the daytime it was fine, because there were always people around, leaving for work, but on one or two occasions she had walked the pavements back to the house on her own and then the sound of her footsteps clattering on the tarmac had made her nervously turn her walk into a semi-run. Good job she didn't suffer from high blood pressure or it would have been through the roof by now. And with winter swiftly descending, the nights would get darker earlier and eight-thirty would seem like midnight. She would have to make an effort not to think about it. 'I like the exercise,' she lied feebly. 'And the fresh air.'

'Because I could always arrange for Jo to drive you home.'

'No!' She was already indebted to Kane for her job, which was far more highly paid, she was sure, than she could have got somewhere else, and for the babysitting which she enjoyed and which, incidentally, further boosted her income. She didn't need to be further reliant on him for her transport. 'I mean, thanks very much but, no, thank you.'

'Why not?'

'Because it would…confuse my arrangements.'

'What arrangements?'

'Arrangements to go somewhere else once I leave your place!' Shannon insisted in a shrill voice, racking her brains to think of any arrangements she had made recently that had involved her not returning in a semi-run back to her dreary bedsit.

'You mean like another fun club,' he said gravely, and she bristled at his patronising tone.

'I shall have to try out quite a few before I find the right one!' she declared defiantly. 'I'm new to the area, after all.'

'A club crawl at nine p.m. on a weekday every time you leave my place. Sounds hard work. Are you sure you're going to be able to fit all this in with getting up in the morning to come to work?'

'I would never let my personal life affect my working life—' Shannon began swiftly, only to be cut down in mid-self-righteous explanation.

'I'm surprised you can say that after your fling with Eric Gallway, which ended up in your leaving your last job and fleeing Ireland.'

That, she thought, was hitting below the belt and she could tell from Kane's sudden flush of discomfort that he was aware of that as well.

'Which is why I shall always make sure that the two sides don't meet,' Shannon retorted. 'Now, will this be all?' She cocked her head to one side in a businesslike manner and he grinned and lowered his eyes. There was a certain wickedness to his grin, she thought absent-mindedly, that belied the stern appearance. Was he aware of that or was it just some characteristic he had been born with? Like some people were born to have dimples when they smiled?

'For the moment,' he agreed, back to his usual highly professional and unreadable self. 'Dennis Clark and one of our accountants will be here in an hour. Make sure there's coffee, would you?'

'Of course, sir,' Shannon said in a docile voice. 'Anything else? Some biscuits perhaps? I could rustle something up from the canteen.' Me secretary, you boss. This was more like it. At the risk of overplaying her role, she was tempted to launch into a selection of various other secretarial duties he might avail himself of, but instead she headed back to the safety of her own office and decided to banish all thoughts of Kane Lindley the man by working fast and furiously and keeping her eyes fixed on the computer screen in front of her.

She was the perfect secretary until lunchtime when she bolted down to the canteen, later than usual because the meeting, in which she'd been asked to sit and take notes, had lasted until after one.

A bowl of soup, some bread and fruit and a cup of coffee, she thought, sitting at one of the many empty tables, would revive her enough for the afternoon. Working for Kane outside work hours had seemed easy enough when she'd accepted the job. How had she known that she would begin to feel a little too submerged in him and his personal life for her own sense of well-being? Eleanor was a joy to look after, but she chattered about her father, whom she adored, and Shannon was finding herself going down the slippery slope of piecing together all the intriguing facets of Kane's personality that emerged during their girlish conversations together after school.

The fact that the women he had brought back to the house, far from being a heady stream of dizzy blondes, had all been, as far as Eleanor had been concerned, boring and formal. Which Shannon shrewdly interpreted as career-women who had found it difficult to accommodate an eight-year-old. The fact that Carrie had developed a crush on him and it had been his idea to relieve her of some of her hours rather than the other way around, which was what he had initially implied.

'How on earth do you know that?' Shannon had laughed.

'I could tell,' was Eleanor's implacable reply. 'She started giggling whenever he was around and finding all sorts of reasons to stay later than she needed to.'

Shannon learnt that Kane rarely took holidays, and when he did he was always in contact with his office, which made her feel acutely sorry for Eleanor, but was firmly told, as a follow-on, that he couldn't help working so hard because it was all to do with looking after her.

She was reflecting on all of this, drinking her soup and relaxing, when a familiar voice said from behind her, 'Mind if I join you?' Before she could answer, Kane slid into the chair opposite her and deposited his plate of salad in front of him and his glass of water.

'What are you doing here?' Shannon muttered, looking around her nervously, relieved that there was no one she recognised left in the canteen. Little did he know that there were quite a few young girls in the company who considered him a heartthrob, and the last thing she needed was the job of fending off their curiosity should they see them together, having lunch.

Then she decided that she was being utterly ridiculous because there was nothing meaningful about sitting at the same table at the same time by chance. Bosses frequently came down to the canteen at lunchtime and most of them sat at whatever table was available, usually at the ones where their secretaries were sitting, which was an instant gossip-quencher but did promote a healthy informality in the company.

'Eating lunch,' he said mildly, pausing in mid-mouthful to look at her. 'And don't look so shocked. I do occasionally manage to slip in a mouthful of food some time during the day.'

'But *here*?'

'If you recall, you suggested I eat here now and again so that I could be on the ground floor when it came to seeing and hearing what's going on in the company.' He gave her one of those bland smiles which she was sincerely coming to distrust. 'Not that there's anyone around to speak of,' he said ruefully. 'Bad timing, I suppose. You're not eating your soup. You can't afford to lose weight. You'll disappear. So eat up.'

Shannon reluctantly swallowed a mouthful of soup while he dug with hearty enthusiasm into his salad, spearing the tiger prawns and making favourable remarks about the quality of the food, finally hinting that maybe he should make the time to frequent the canteen a bit more often, and when it was more crowded.

'You can't!' Shannon squeaked.

'Why not?' His dark eyes were unrevealing which, she thought sceptically, meant that he would somehow try and worm a response out of her by feigning innocence. Since she wasn't about to comply, she started talking briskly about work, meanwhile drinking her soup as rapidly as she could without spilling the lot in the process.

After she had concluded her five-minute monologue on various assorted topics, ranging from the filing system to computer programs, he looked at her calmly and said, 'I get the impression that you're a little on edge. I hope I haven't unsettled you in any way by joining you for lunch.'

'Unsettle me? Of course not!' She laughed to further the impression that it would be impossible for him to unsettle her, then laughed again just in case he hadn't received the first message. 'Why on earth would I be unsettled by you?'

Kane shrugged his broad shoulders and continued eating. If he was at ease with the silence stretching like elastic between them, she certainly wasn't. What on earth was wrong with her? She could hear herself babbling about everything under the sun until she finally ran out of steam, at which point he surprised her by asking about Christmas.

'Christmas? What about it?' Shannon asked, bewildered.

'What are you doing about it? Going back to Ireland? Staying here? The reason I ask is because Eleanor would like you to spend Christmas with us if you're at a loose end.'

Spend Christmas with them? He really must feel very sorry for her! Fortunately, she had already planned on heading back to her family for Christmas so she could reject his offer in all truthfulness.

'I really would have enjoyed that,' she told him, laying it on thick, 'but I've already told my mum that I'll be back home for Christmas. The family have never spent Christmas apart, not even when Francis was away studying in Paris. I'm sorry. I'll explain it to Eleanor, if you like.'

'No, I'll do that. She'll be disappointed, of course.'

'Haven't you got…grandparents? Aunts? Cousins?'

'We're a small family. Pretty much the opposite of yours. Now. Back to work, I suppose. Although I rather fancy playing truant at the moment.' He chuckled at the thought of it.

She said, startled at the personal aside, 'I can't imagine you playing truant.'

'It seems there are quite a number of things you can't imagine me doing,' he said, ticking them off on his fingers. 'Playing truant, gyrating on a dance floor, eating lunch...would you like me to tell you what I can't imagine *you* doing?'

'Not really,' Shannon said hurriedly, alarmed at this sudden turn in the conversation, and he laughed as though her response had been exactly as he'd predicted. He was no psychic but he had a knack of seeming to second guess her reactions which she found a little unnerving. Either he was a sharp judge of human character or else her human character was so bland and transparent that he could read her like a book.

'I just couldn't imagine what,' she informed him coldly, 'you would do if you did play truant. Go to the park and feed the ducks? Take in a sneaky afternoon movie? Head for the nearest junk-food place and gorge yourself on hamburgers?' There. That sarcasm should put him in his place if nothing else.

'I like the park option,' Kane said slowly, undeterred by her tone of voice. He stood up, waiting till she clambered to her feet, then they strolled back to the bank of lifts, with Shannon looking shiftily around her just in case someone she knew appeared in front of her like a rabbit from a magician's hat. 'A leisurely walk in the park...'

'It's freezing outside,' she pointed out with crushing pragmatism.

'True. Point taken. Then perhaps in a cabin some-where in front of a roaring fire.'

The image sent a little shiver down her spine as her imagination took flight once again into the land of no-go.

'I never thought truants liked skipping work for that kind of thing,' she told him, watching as he punched a button to the side of the lifts and they waited for one to arrive. 'Anyway, why don't you just take some time off and go away somewhere with Eleanor?'

The lift arrived and they stepped inside. As the door shut, Shannon had a sudden trapped feeling and found herself pressed against the back, staring fixedly ahead of her but very much aware of the man slightly in front.

'Time is the one thing I never seem to have enough of,' he commented drily.

'Which would make a depressing epitaph,' she said lightly. 'Why don't you do something about it? In fact, in a couple of weeks' time Eleanor's class is putting on a play. Nothing formally to do with Christmas...' Shannon smiled as she remembered this particular con-versation '...since there are several religious denomi-nations to be considered. It's at two in the afternoon, before school finishes. She'd be thrilled if she knew you were going.'

The lift finally arrived at their floor and as the doors opened Kane leant against one so she could slide past. Out of the claustrophobic confines of the lift, she could feel her treacherous breathing return to normal.

'Were you planning on going to this play?' he asked, and Shannon blushed.

'I might have the afternoon off,' she admitted. 'It broke my heart to think of the little mite in a play with no family or friends to watch. At eight, children get so excited about things like that. It's a shame.'

'What else does Eleanor get excited about that she fails to mention?'

A good eight inches shorter than him, Shannon had to walk at a brisk pace to keep up with his long, easy strides, and by the time they were back at her office she was slightly out of breath.

She shrugged noncommittally and sat down, putting on her supposedly stern secretarial mask. But instead of going away, he swung her chair round so that she was facing him and placed his hands squarely on either side of her. The jittery claustrophobia she felt now made those few minutes in the lift seem like a run in the open countryside by comparison.

'Care to answer my question?' he pressed, towering over her, his tie falling forward to brush against her blouse.

'Oh, just the usual. She's got a starring role in this production. Apparently, it's a great honour not to be sidelined into playing one of the animals. She's thrilled because she has a speaking part and Jodie, the class big-mouth, is playing a camel.' Shannon grinned. 'She's also excited because she's now in the top group in maths and her poem was read out day before yesterday at assembly in front of the lower years.'

Kane looked bemused by this array of accomplishments.

'It's not my fault I have to work all the hours God made,' he objected roughly, as if she had criticised his parenting. A bad case of guilty conscience, she decided, and well deserved as well.

'It *is* your fault, actually. You could make more time

for Eleanor, and don't tell me about your weekends. You constantly get business calls on a Sunday, anyway!'

'Business calls! On the weekend!' He was virtually spluttering.

'Yes,' Shannon said smugly. 'Eleanor told me. Girls' talk.'

'And what else do you girls talk about when I'm not around?'

'I can make sure that you're free for the play. Will you be coming? As I said to you, Eleanor *would be thrilled.*'

He pushed himself back from her chair and appraised her with his eyes. 'I wouldn't dream of missing it, now that it's been brought to my attention. Nor,' he added, shoving his hands into his pockets and smiling with satisfaction, 'would I dream of letting you miss it. Not after you had planned on going. I think this mighty corporation could do without us for a couple of hours, don't you? We can watch Eleanor in the play and then afterwards we can take her out for something to eat somewhere. Settled?' He flashed her one of those smiles that indicated there was no room for manoeuvre.

One week later, Shannon was feeling even more hopelessly ensnared. Ensnared on a stake of her own making. And helpless to protest because Kane's new-found determination to put her advice into practice and see more of his daughter was all to the good. At least all to the good as far as Eleanor was concerned. She was probably seeing more of her father during the weekdays than she had for her entire life. Shannon left him working at five only to see him again at six-thirty when he strolled through the front door to delighted squeals from his daughter. And more disastrous to her mental health than that, he always insisted that she join them for supper.

'She's so thrilled at you being here with us,' he'd told her depressingly on the first evening of his run of early homecomings. 'She really almost considers you to be one of the family.'

'But I'm *not* one of the family!' Shannon had protested vigorously, her hands on her hips, glaring at him as he'd divested himself of his jacket and moved away, tugging at his tie to remove it and drape it over the banister. 'I happen to have my *own* family!'

'But they're not here, are they?' he had countered smugly.

'I'm not looking for a family substitute!'

'And I'm not offering you one. I'm merely suggesting that it seems so important to Eleanor, and what's important to Eleanor is important to me.'

Which had silenced her. He'd seemed so sincere, almost vulnerable in the admission, but a healthy sceptical streak in her read that as a cunning move to get what he wanted and there was no denying that it was easier for him when she was around. He could relax, have a drink and whilst he was bombarded with Eleanor's accounts of school and what had happened that day, a fair amount of time was spent comfortably watching his daughter and Shannon play games, cook tea and exchange ideas while he sat at the kitchen table, making the occasional remark and half reading the newspapers.

The domesticity of it frightened her, but when she tried to dig deeper into the reasons for that, she came up against a brick wall.

Now, as she slung on her coat and braced herself to face the brisk walk to the underground and the tube journey back to her bedsit, she couldn't help looking at him accusingly from under her lashes.

'What?' he asked, walking her to the front door and

muttering that he didn't care for the thought of her journeying back to her bedsit in the dark.

'I didn't say anything.'

'You don't have to. You're like an angry little bull terrier waiting for a leg to bite. My leg, I get the feeling.'

'I'm not *little*,' Shannon told him through gritted teeth. 'And I'm not a child either.'

'You look like a child with those pigtails. Why do you tie your hair back all the time?'

'It's practical,' Shannon said uncomfortably. She self-consciously took one of her ridiculous braids in one hand and played with it. Lots of women wore their hair tied back! 'And I can't wear it tied back in a bun because it's not long enough. Not that I have to explain my hairstyles to you.'

She thought of one of the company lawyers who made a habit of popping in unannounced and insisting on seeing Kane with important business. A tall, glamorous blonde with fashionably short hair. She doubted whether Kane had ever mentioned to her that she looked like a tomboy with such short hair!

'I suppose I could have it all chopped off, like Sonya Crew,' she added waspishly. 'Would that be mature enough for your liking?'

He gave her a long, leisurely and very thorough look which sent shivers down her spine, and she edged back against the front door. 'Anyway, I've got to go,' she said in confusion. 'I don't want to be getting back too late.'

'Which has been my point all along,' he said mildly, still looking at her with that shuttered expression that sent her nervous system into panicky overdrive. 'How long will it take you to get back?'

'Oh, about half an hour, I guess. Maybe a little more.' If she pushed any harder against the wooden door she would go right through it, but for some reason she felt threatened by Kane's proximity and, worse, excited by the thought of it.

He stepped back. 'Right. I'll see you tomorrow, if you're sure you don't want to be driven back.'

Shannon heard herself squeak out a stuttering refusal.

'And tomorrow there's no need for you to come after work,' he continued. 'I'm going to be back late so Carrie's staying on for the night. You can catch up on your social life which must have gone into a bit of decline with the hours you've been putting in here.'

'Oh, no. As I said, I leave here early enough to go out afterwards!'

She felt disproportionately disappointed to be missing that little illicit taste of domesticity which she now found she had become pleasurably accustomed to. Reactions like that wouldn't do and she immediately decided that she would go to the pub after work with some of the girls from the office. She couldn't afford to pander to her instincts to behave like the homebody she naturally was. She would just find herself slipping into another rut, this time involving a family that wasn't hers.

She was young and living in the Big City! It was crucial that she remind herself of the fact, and of the fact that she should be out there enjoying all the wonderfully exciting things that London had to offer after dark. One brief foray into a second-rate nightclub didn't really qualify her to join the ranks of the young and free, did it? And cosy meals with Sandy didn't count either. Starting from next week, she would dictate the days she babysat for him and start concentrating on herself.

'In fact,' she said boldly, pleased with the various options she had now opened for herself, 'tomorrow suits me. I'll go to the pub with some girls from work, maybe head for a club after—'

'Head for a club? On a Tuesday?'

'That's right!' Shannon snapped. 'I can party till dawn and not feel the effects!'

She gave him a challenging look and then considered that she had scored a point when he was the first to look away, opening the door for her with his usual gentlemanly politeness. She'd discovered that he belonged to that old-fashioned and sadly fast-disappearing breed of men who still believed in treating women like ladies.

The opposite of Eric Gallway, in fact, who had once remarked, sniggering at his own sense of dubious humour, that women shouldn't expect to be treated any differently from men since they all seemed to make such a fuss about being equal, and since when did he ever open doors for men? It hadn't occurred to her at the time to counter that by asking him why, then, he bought her chocolates and flowers.

But maybe, in the throes of her infatuation, she might not have cared for the obvious answer, which would have been that chocolates and flowers were groundwork for getting a woman into bed.

'Lucky to be so young and carefree,' he murmured blandly, giving her one of those smiles that suggested the opposite of what he was actually saying but left no room to argue the toss.

'I think so!' she threw back carelessly. 'Now, if you don't mind…?'

But the following day, Shannon couldn't help but wonder whether she'd had a victory over him at all. She also found that going to the pub wasn't the attractive option she had banked on. In fact, a malicious inner voice told her, it was decidedly inferior to babysitting

Eleanor and waiting in tense expectation of Kane's arrival.

At eight-thirty, she found that she was restlessly looking at her watch and rather than continue to cradle her glass, she drained it, made her excuses and began the journey back to the bedsit.

It was now dark by four in the afternoon and by nine it was dark enough and cold enough for her to think that she was walking down some street in Siberia. A stiff, steady breeze whipped against her, making her ears and face and fingers feel numb.

From the underground to her place was no more than a matter of fifteen minutes' walk. She made it back in under ten, racing along the pavements, her arms tightly drawn around her body to conserve some heat.

It occurred to her that when she had decided to flee Ireland and head for another life in London, she could just have easily have headed abroad. Somewhere hot. She could have got a job doing a spot of nannying somewhere where the sun shone until eight in the evening. Or, frankly, somewhere where the sun shone and didn't pay occasional visits like a guest with better things to do than hang around in one spot for too long. The Italian Riviera might have been nice. She might have had to learn Italian but it would have been a small sacrifice for glorious warm days and glamorous movie-star-style nights, flitting from one venue to another.

The fantasy was enough to sustain her sense of humour until she made it back to her bedsit, clambering up the three flights of stairs to the shabby door to her room. She couldn't wait to feed the meter and get some heat crawling back into her.

What a dump, Shannon thought, looking around her despondently. She was sick and tired of trying to see the good things about it. The fact that it was fairly central and not too far from the underground. The fact that the fridge and stove and oven actually worked. The fact that, unlike most bedsits, this one had its own bathroom. Was it any wonder, she asked herself fiercely, that she was so willing to work extra hours, babysitting?

It was nine-thirty by the time the room had warmed up sufficiently for her to relax. She'd had a shower and changed into her maiden-aunt night attire of flannel nightdress and fluffy bedroom slippers. She'd had nothing to eat but the thought of doing anything that required more effort than it took to make a mug of hot chocolate wasn't worth thinking about. Another thing, she thought sourly, that she had become accustomed to. Hot food, the shared pleasure of making it with Eleanor.

To begin with, Mrs Porter had left casseroles for them to eat, but after a couple of days they had both found it more fun to try their hand at cooking dinner themselves. There were always masses of fresh vegetables and the freezer was well stocked. Mrs Porter, who did all the shopping, was as expert in her purchasing as she evidently was in her culinary skills.

She switched on the television and was half watching something on the news when there was a knock on the door. Three sharp knocks, actually. Since Shannon couldn't imagine who it could be, and there was no way that she was opening the door to some drunken lout who had come to see someone else in the building and had mistakenly lurched his way to her door instead, she remained where she was, cradling her mug with her hands, her feet curled under her, waiting for whoever it might be to stagger off to their correct destination. When the knocking continued, but more urgently, she finally stormed to the door and flung it open. Or rather flung it open the few inches that her chain lock permitted.

'Mind letting me in?' Kane asked.

She didn't. She was too shocked to see him. 'Who's with Eleanor? What are you doing here?'

'Mrs Porter. Let me in.'

'How did you know where I lived?'

'These and other questions to be answered shortly. Just as soon as you open this door and let me in.'

CHAPTER FIVE

'WAIT a minute.' Before Kane could say anything, Shannon slammed the door in his face and rushed to get her bathrobe.

She reappeared at the door several seconds later with the bathrobe drawn tightly around her. The bedroom slippers, a previous Christmas present from one of her brothers, would have to stay on.

'Come in, then,' she said reluctantly, pulling back the chain and allowing him to enter.

'How,' she asked, leaning against the door with her hands behind her while he took the few steps needed to get to the other side of the room, 'did you know my address?'

He was so damned big that her bedsit seemed to have shrunk to the size of a matchbox, and his masculine aroma, a fuzzy mixture of clean, cold air and the remnants of aftershave, filled her nostrils like incense.

'I know everything, reds. Haven't you realised that already?' He grinned. 'Actually, I had a look in your personnel file. Believe it or not, that's what they're there for. Useful information. And stop standing by that door and shivering. Why don't you offer me something to drink? Like a good hostess would.'

'It's late. I really am tired.'

'I thought you said that you could party from dusk till dawn,' he pointed out, using her own frivolous aside to bludgeon through her feeble excuse. 'Mind if I take my coat off?'

82

Shannon shrugged in a non-answer and he removed the trench coat, folding it in half and then placing it on one of the two chairs in the room.

'Ah. Hot chocolate,' he said, spying the half-empty cup on the table. 'It's been years since I had hot chocolate. I used to love it when I was a kid. A cup would be great.' He gave her a slow, implacable smile and Shannon reluctantly unglued herself from the door and sidled past him, muttering along the way that he might as well sit down and make himself comfortable.

She returned a few minutes later with a mug of hot chocolate to find him browsing unashamedly among the array of family snapshots which had been the first thing to decorate her bedsit when she'd first moved in.

'Who's this?' he asked, holding up a framed picture in one hand.

'My family,' Shannon said, handing him the mug but keeping her distance.

'Brothers and sisters?'

'Yes.'

'What are their names?'

So she had to take a few steps closer to him to peer at the picture and point to each member of her family, listing them by name from the eldest Shaun down to the youngest Brian. As she spoke, he sipped his hot chocolate and she could feel his breath as he exhaled very gently on the top of her head. When she had finished, he carefully placed the picture on the ledge exactly where he had found it, but continued to scan them all, asking her questions about where they were now and what they were doing.

'You must be very close to them.'

'I am.'

'Which is probably why you're such a natural when

it comes to Eleanor. You've grown accustomed over the years to sharing your time with other people. What about your father?'

'He died a few years ago.'

'I'm sorry to hear that,' Kane said quietly.

He moved back but instead of sitting in the required docile manner on the chair so that she could begin quizzing him on what he was doing in her bedsit at this time of the night, he surveyed the rest of the room, even having the nerve to check the kitchen, before saying with a frown, 'Where's the bedroom?'

'Why?' Shannon immediately asked with sudden, mounting panic. 'Why do you want to know where the bedroom is?'

'*Bedroom* I said, not *bed*.' He gave the chair in the corner a doubtful look, as if unsure as to whether it would take his weight, and then gingerly sat down.

'There is no bedroom. The sofa is really a single bed. I just fling the sheet on it when I'm ready to go to bed and use the big, square cushions for pillows. It's very comfy, actually.'

'You sleep on a chair?'

'Sofa,' she corrected, bristling at the incredulous contempt in his voice at her living arrangements.

'Surely we pay you enough to find somewhere a bit...' he looked around him and she could see him searching for the least offensive description to apply '...bigger?'

'Places are very hard to come by in London,' Shannon informed him, following his eyes and looking around the poky room herself. 'It was a bit of luck getting this in the first place, as a matter of fact.'

'Yes. A bit of bad luck.' Kane drank some more of the hot chocolate. 'How was your evening at the pub?'

'Don't try to distract me with lots of questions. What are you doing here?'

'I was in the area and...'

'You thought you'd drop by for a cup of coffee and a chat?'

'Not exactly, no. I thought I'd take a drive to see how far you have to walk once you get to your underground station here.'

Shannon gave an exasperated sigh.

'And I wanted to check out the area,' he expanded, making her feel even more cringingly helpless.

'Is there any chance at all that you might stop acting as though I'm too young or too stupid to take care of myself?' Realising that she was still standing up, Shannon tucked herself back into the sofa and folded her arms imperiously.

'If that's the impression I've given you, I apologise,' he said in a voice that didn't sound very apologetic, 'but when I think of Eleanor living in a place like this, my skin crawls. And if, for some reason, she found herself forced to, I'd be bloody glad if there was someone around who took an interest.'

'You mean someone like you.'

Kane shrugged and raised his eyebrows.

'In other words, I should be grateful for you nosing around in my private life.'

'Does your mother know about your living conditions?' he asked shrewdly, and Shannon squirmed a little bit, whilst trying to hang on to the liberated, twenty-first century veneer she was in the process of creating.

'Of course she does,' Shannon lied. It was, in fact, such a vast lie, that she amended slightly, 'Well, she knows I don't live anywhere grand...' She had an uncomfortable feeling that her mum thought she was living somewhere small but charming, a bit like a smaller version of her own house, in fact. Somewhere with more than two rooms and an atmosphere of cosy homeliness. She would have an instant heart attack were she to know that the small but charming place in her head was in reality a charmless dump in a borderline part of the city.

Shannon could imagine her mother swooping down to London on a bedsit inspection tour and she would probably drag her daughter back off to Ireland the minute she clapped eyes on her rented accommodation.

'I take it you've been economical with the truth.'

'I had to,' Shannon grumbled defensively, 'for her own good.'

He didn't say anything for so long that she finally blurted out, 'Look, I haven't eaten yet, so would you mind leaving? I'm tired and I'm hungry and I'm not in the mood to argue with you. I'm not your child, you don't have to look after me and when I can afford something better, I shall naturally move out. I don't see why you're complaining. I do a good job for you at work and I don't complain about travelling back here in the evenings.'

'Why haven't you eaten?'

Oh, Lord, here we go again, she thought. More lectures, this time about the importance of nutrition.

'Because I was having such a brilliant time at the pub that I just didn't give it a moment's thought!'

'Well, we'd better rectify the situation.' He stood up and Shannon scrambled to her feet in pursuit.

'"We'd" better rectify the situation?'

'That's right.' He began rummaging through her cupboards, then he opened the fridge and scanned the contents with a critical eye.

'Not much here, is there?'

'Do you mind?' Shannon spluttered to his back, finally slipping past him and slamming the fridge door shut.

The fridge, as she had known, was virtually bare. No cheese, just some butter and some milk, but whoever heard of spaghetti and milk? Or spaghetti and chocolate mousse? With a few mouldy onions thrown in for good measure?

She closed the fridge door and faced him with quiet dignity.

'I may have forgotten do go shopping recently,' she agreed loftily, catching his amused eye for a few seconds then looking away. 'As a matter of fact, I've never been one of these people who is obsessed with food.'

'I wouldn't call having more than three items in a fridge being *obsessed with food*,' he murmured. 'Go and get changed, reds, and we'll go out and have a quick meal. 'I'll turn my back while you get dressed, if you like,' he added gallantly, and she snorted with laughter.

'OK, then, I won't.' He looked at her slowly, from her feet upwards, taking his time, arms folded, until every nerve in her body was vibrating with tension.

'I don't suppose you'll just go away?'

'Now, why would I do that when I can stand here and watch you change?' He smiled at her blushing outrage as she pulled open the door to the small wardrobe, wretchedly conscious of the man peering curiously over her shoulder. She extracted the first things that came to hand and stormed into the bathroom, locking the door behind her.

'No need to lock the door, you know,' his voice came from very close to the door indeed. 'Don't you trust me?'

'You're a man, aren't you?' Shannon retorted, struggling out of one set of clothes and into another—this time jeans, a long-sleeved green jumper and a pair of thick socks.

'Now, why do I get the feeling that underneath that liberated, feminist remark is an incurable romantic?'

'Because,' she said, yanking the door open and, as she'd expected, finding him standing two inches away from it, 'you don't know me?'

Instead of answering, Kane located her coat hanging from a hook behind the door and held it out for her. The brief contact of his fingers brushing against her arms felt strangely like an invasion of her privacy and she stepped away, fumbling with the buttons, aware that in her haste to get dressed she had omitted a bra, so that now her breasts felt heavy and her nipples tingled against the rough grain of the jumper. She had a fleeting reckless thought that he might very well be aware of her bra-less state, and hot on the heels of that came the even more reckless thought of his hands caressing her bare breasts under the jumper, seeking out her sensitive nipples, playing with them with his fingers. Just imagining it, it made her body feel hot and feverish.

'I hope I'm well dressed enough for this little meal you've insisted on taking me for.' She had thought that a sparky comment from her might re-create some vital distance between them but, instead of rising to her bait, he smiled and raised his eyebrows in an unnervingly knowing way.

'It makes a delightful change to see you out of work clothes,' he said, opening her door and then politely stepping back so that she could fiddle with her key.

'*Delightful?* Isn't that taking courtesy a bit far?' she asked feverishly.

'Don't you like being described as delightful?' His

eyes were shuttered. 'What adjective would you rather I used? How about sexy? Mmm. Yes, sexy might be more apt. Those freckles, that ivory white skin and flaming hair. Not obviously sexy, but discreetly so. Like a woman in jeans and a man's shirt, not thinking she's flaunting anything but arousing all sorts of illicit thoughts anyway.'

His words made her feel limp.

'I don't arouse illicit thoughts,' she squeaked.

'How do you know?'

'Because...' she spluttered helplessly.

'Would it turn you on if you thought you did?'

'No!'

'So...should I keep my illicit thoughts to myself, then?' He dropped his eyes so that she couldn't see whether he was being serious or not. No, of course he wasn't being serious, she thought hotly.

'You haven't got any illicit thoughts, so you can stop playing games!'

'You're very suspicious of the opposite sex, aren't you?' he said, letting her off the hook and allowing her to lead the way down the narrow flight of stairs to the front door, but stepping forward once they were in the hall to open the door for her. 'Not really surprising, I suppose. One sour relationship can have a knock-on effect that lasts much longer than we expect.'

'Oh, you speak from experience, do you?' Shannon asked sarcastically, stepping past him, her head held high just in case he got the notion that anything he said might actually be absorbed and stored for inspection at a later date.

'Not really, no,' he admitted, walking towards the high street, his hands in his pockets and his coat flapping around him, brushing against her legs. They walked with their heads down, instinctively pushing against the bracing wind that had sent the temperatures dropping.

'Was that what Gallway asked you to do? Trust him?' he quizzed her shrewdly, and Shannon could have kicked herself for her momentary slip of the tongue.

'Isn't that what *all* men say when they're intent on getting a woman into bed?' Shannon retorted heatedly.

'No, actually.'

'*You're* different, I suppose?'

'Very different,' he murmured. 'Look. There. A Chinese restaurant. Shall we try it?'

'OK,' she said grudgingly. 'I never noticed before, not that I spend much time on the high street.'

'Too dull?'

'Way too dull for someone as sizzling as I am,' she answered brashly. 'Not enough...pubs and wine bars and swinging clubs.'

At which Kane had the insufferable temerity to burst out laughing, and she felt a smile reluctantly tug the corners of her mouth. Like it or not, she was enjoying his company, even though he had dragged her out of the warmth of her room at an ungodly hour, kicking and screaming, more or less.

'London isn't just about pubs and wine bars and swinging clubs,' he pointed out. 'What about the theatres, the operas, the restaurants, the art galleries, the museums?'

'What about them?' Shannon shot back airily. She decided that she would get some fun out of the remainder of the evening after all and play him at his own game of being patronising. She brushed past him as he held open the door for her to enter the restaurant, which was not quite empty but nearly.

'What do you mean ''what about them?'''

'Well…' She allowed herself to be relieved of her coat and then waited until she had sat down at the small table. 'Yes, there *is* the theatre,' she agreed, ticking off option one on her finger. 'But if I could afford constant trips to the theatre I would have enough money to move out of that hole I call home away from home, wouldn't I?'

'So you *do* admit that it's a hole.'

'But I never said I didn't like living in holes. Some people do, you know.'

'Ah, I see. Or do I?' He grinned and waited for her to continue.

'Then the opera. Well, really. I would have to save three months' pay to afford a seat at an opera.'

'Not quite three months.'

'Besides, I hate opera.'

'Have you ever been?'

'No. So that's the opera taken care of. Then the restaurants. I worked in one so actually going to one always felt like a busman's holiday.' She ticked off that particular option. 'Then the art galleries and museums. Very interesting, I'm sure. Very cultured and refined, but—'

'Don't say it—you're a wild young thing with no time for culture and refinement…'

'I'm glad you noticed! Perhaps,' she added wickedly, 'when I'm older and more mature…'

'Like me…'

'If the cap fits…' She smiled smugly at him and then proceeded to inspect her menu. A pointless exercise as she allowed him to order the food rather than wade her way through everything on the menu. 'I mean…' she leaned towards him with her elbows resting on the table '…in between your operas, theatres, museums and art galleries, don't you sometimes just long for the hectic buzz of a club?'

He appeared to give that some thought, stroking his chin with one finger, looking at her with a pensive expression that didn't quite conceal the humour lurking just beneath the surface. 'Is there a hectic buzz in a club? I thought it was all loud music and drunken youths.'

'See!' Shannon exclaimed triumphantly.

'What am I supposed to have seen? Oh, I know. That I'm an old fuddy-duddy? A stick-in-the-mud? I *do* manage to get out now and again to the old club, actually. Sorry to disappoint you.' He sat back to allow the waiter to pour them both a glass of wine while Shannon digested the image of Kane Lindley flinging himself around on a dance floor in hip-gripping snakeskin trousers and garish top. It was almost easier to imagine him in a black frock and dog collar preaching from a pulpit.

'You go to clubs?' she asked, guzzling her wine like water and giving him a patronising, incredulous smirk.

'Admittedly not the kind of clubs you probably have in mind.'

'Oh, you mean dreary gentlemen's clubs where you all sit around little table sipping glasses of sherry and discussing politics...'

'Not quite.'

'Then what kind of clubs are you talking about?' The cold white wine tasted glorious, although with nothing in her stomach Shannon could feel the alcohol racing through her bloodstream and shooting straight to her brain.

'Jazz clubs, for the most part.'

'Oh, jazz.'

'Another piece of culture you find you have no time for, by any chance?' He refilled her now empty glass and sat back to look at her. How was it possible for anyone still dressed in their working garb to look so cool and unflappable at this time of evening? Not to mention bright-eyed and bushy-tailed?

'Not really exciting, are they? All slow music and sensible conversation...'

'Depends who you go with.' He raised his glass to his lips and looked at her with amusement over the rim while she went a delicate shade of pink.

'I doubt that very much,' Shannon declared robustly, uncomfortably aware that the image of Kane dancing very slowly, cheek to cheek, with a woman at a jazz club made her feel more bothered than she would have admitted in a million years. There had been no evidence of any women in his life, at least not since she'd been around, working for him, and he'd been increasingly at the house whenever she'd been there in the evenings during the week. But what did that say? His weekends could be spent anywhere. He could have a woman for every weekend for all she knew.

'Do you? Why? Don't you think that listening to good music and dancing to it can be a very erotic experience?'

'I prefer dancing to quicker numbers myself,' Shannon told him quickly, relieved that their food had now arrived, conveniently marking an end to this particular line of conversation, even though she knew that she had generated it in the first place. She watched him surreptitiously as she helped herself to food, ravenously hungry all of a sudden.

'Have you ever been to a jazz club?' he asked, once they had begun eating.

'Not really.' She manoeuvred her chopsticks around a mouthful of cashew chicken and noodles and hoped that the food would soak up some of the wine which had made her feel pleasantly but unreliably light-headed.

'What does ''not really'' mean?'

'It means no, actually.'

'Oh, dear. No jazz clubs, no opera, nothing that smacks of culture.'

'As a matter of fact, I would *love* to go to jazz clubs and theatres and I might even be persuaded to try the opera...' Unlikely, that last one, she thought, but who could tell? 'But these things cost money which I haven't got at my ready disposal. Unfortunately.' She could feel herself warming to her theme of misplaced cultured person, just in case he imagined that she was a bimbo whose only interest was to go somewhere where the maximum amount of sweat could be worked up in the minimum amount of time. In fact, the few nightclubs she had frequented in her lifetime had left a lot to be desired. That, however, was a little titbit she would not be sharing with him.

'I can't think of anything more exciting,' she ventured, realising with some surprise that she had drunk three glasses of wine and eaten enough food to keep her going for a month, 'than going to...the Tate Gallery, followed by an evening at a quiet, refined club. Just grabbing an exquisite meal somewhere along the way, of course! It would be wonderful to...' Her mind was beginning to feel decidedly fuzzy.

'To...?' Kane prompted silkily.

Where was she? Oh, yes. She was in the middle of conjuring up an alternative lifestyle as befitted someone whose proclivities were more in tune with culture, and not culture of the youth variety. 'To really wear something fancy to go out...a little black number...or maybe something elegant...and backless...in dark green...'

'You have little black numbers and elegant, backless dark green frocks?'

'*Frocks?* No one uses that word nowadays.'

'You fall for it every time, don't you,' Kane murmured, watching her from under his lashes. 'Have you?'

'Have I what?' *Fall for what every time?*

'Got fancy dresses with no place to wear them?'

Having embarked on this road, Shannon suspected that ignominiously admitting a complete lack of any such thing would make all her protests of wanting to absorb culture like the proverbial sponge appear hollow if not a downright lie. And for some perverse reason she wanted to impress him. She wanted to prove that she wasn't just his secretary who was adept at handling his work and good with children, whose only source of amusement were pubs and the odd foray into clubbing. Neither of which had lived up to her expectations anyway.

'Yes,' she lied.

'Mmm. A little black number…'

'That's right! Very little and very black as a matter of fact.'

'The mind boggles. Sure that isn't the wine talking?' he asked with a straight face.

'Quite sure.' Shannon scowled.

'In which case…' He signalled for the bill and looked at her pensively. Too pensively for her liking. She began to feel a little rattled by the lingering silence.

'In which case…*what*?' she demanded impatiently.

'In which case,' he murmured, 'it seems a shame not to have the opportunity to use your glamorous outfits, doesn't it?'

'Just what I've been saying.' Shannon shrugged ruefully, rather pleased with the image she had succeeded in creating for herself. She'd always been the cute, chatty one in the family. The easygoing member upon whom her mother could always rely. Willing to help out in the house, happy to look after the younger ones when her sisters had been too busy rushing about, getting into mad flaps over boys and dates and party dresses. She'd been privileged to have lots of friends of the opposite sex, simply because she'd always been one of the lads. Now, with a few choice phrases and white lies, she had become, she thought gleefully to herself, a woman of mystery and intrigue. She didn't currently feel too mysterious or intriguing in her get-up of jeans and sweater, but in a small, black number she was certain she could be.

'Are we ready to go?' she asked, surprised because she had been having such a good time. When she stood up, she felt slightly giddy and he took her arm.

'Feeling steady enough to walk back?'

'Of course I am. But,' she added slyly, 'if I wasn't, would you do the gentlemanly thing and carry me?'

'That wine has definitely gone to your head,' he muttered under his breath, guiding her along the pavement which was now deserted so that the sound of their footsteps echoed on the concrete.

'You're avoiding the question! Would you carry me?'

'Of course I would,' he said drily, and Shannon laughed.

'And risk three slipped discs in the process?'

'You look as though you'd be as light as a feather,' he told her huskily, and she felt her body flooded with sudden, furious heat at the tone of his voice. 'Would you like me to prove it to you?' He moved round so that he was facing her, and in the darkness she could see mocking challenge in his eyes. He couldn't be serious, could he? It was difficult to tell, especially when the streetlights were throwing his face into sharp angles, making it impossible to decipher any expression.

Play the LUCKY Carnival Wheel Game...

GET YOUR 3 GIFTS FREE !

PLAY FOR FREE ! NO PURCHASE NECESSARY !

How To Play:

1. With a coin, carefully scratch off the 3 gold areas on your Lucky Carnival Wheel. By doing so you have qualified to receive everything revealed—2 FREE books and a surprise gift—ABSOLUTELY FREE!

2. Send back this card and you'll receive 2 brand-new Harlequin Presents® novels. These books have a cover price of $4.25 each in the U.S. and $4.99 each in Canada, but they are yours ABSOLUTELY FREE.

3. There's no catch! You're under no obligation to buy anything. We charge nothing—ZERO—for your first shipment. And you don't have to make any minimum number of purchases— not even one!

4. The fact is thousands of readers enjoy receiving books by mail from the Harlequin Reader Service®. They enjoy the convenience of home delivery...they like getting the best new novels at discount prices, BEFORE they're available in stores... and they love their *Heart to Heart* subscriber newsletter featuring author news, horoscopes, recipes, book reviews and much more!

5. We hope that after receiving your free books you'll want to remain a subscriber. But the choice is yours—to continue or cancel, any time at all! So why not take us up on our invitation, with no risk of any kind. You'll be glad you did!

A surprise gift
FREE
We can't tell you what it is...but we're sure you'll like it! A
FREE GIFT!
just for playing LUCKY CARNIVAL WHEEL!

LUCKY Carnival Wheel

Find Out Instantly The Gifts You Get Absolutely FREE!

Scratch-off Game

Scratch off **ALL 3** Gold areas

YES! I have scratched off the 3 Gold Areas above.

Please send me the 2 FREE books and gift for which I qualify! I understand I am under no obligation to purchase any books, as explained on the back and on the opposite page.

306 HDL DNWT   106 HDL DNWJ

FIRST NAME   LAST NAME

ADDRESS

APT.#   CITY

STATE/PROV.   ZIP/POSTAL CODE

The Harlequin Reader Service® —Here's how it works:

Accepting your 2 free books and gift places you under no obligation to buy anything. You may keep the books and gift and return the shipping statement marked "cancel." If you do not cancel, about a month later we'll send you 6 additional novels and bill you just $3.57 each in the U.S., or $4.24 each in Canada, plus 25¢ shipping & handling per book and applicable taxes if any.* That's the complete price and — compared to cover prices of $4.25 each in the U.S. and $4.99 each in Canada—it's quite a bargain! You may cancel at any time, but if you choose to continue, every month we'll send you 6 more books, which you may either purchase at the discount price or return to us and cancel your subscription.

*Terms and prices subject to change without notice. Sales tax applicable in N.Y. Canadian residents will be charged applicable provincial taxes and GST.

'Believe me, I weigh more than you think.' Shannon felt her breath catch in her throat. 'It's cold, isn't it? If we don't run back I think I might get frostbite.'

'Backing away, Shannon?' he whispered softly, but he moved aside and fell into step with her so that she wondered whether she had imagined all those various disconcerting tones in his voice. More than likely, considering the way her imagination had taken flight after the wine. On impulse, Kane scooped her up in his arms and carried her to the front door while she protested wildly against his chest and tried to flail her arms and legs, to no avail.

'Put me down!' she wailed eventually, when they were at her front door.

'All in good time. Now, why don't you get your key out of your bag and open up the front door for us?'

'I can't like this!' She was clutching her bag to her chest, using it as a flimsy barrier between herself and his broad chest.

'Give it a try.'

She frantically unzipped her bag and pulled out her bunch of keys, which he promptly took from her with one hand so that he could open the door without putting her down. Moving against him made her skin burn with a strange, restless heat, and where his arms curled behind her back, reaching to grasp around her behind the bent crook of her knees and her chest, it made her want to writhe in a useless attempt to escape. His fingers were splayed only inches from the curve of her breast and her head was consumed with graphic images of them touching her soft flesh. Even if only accidentally.

'That's quite enough,' she protested giddily, as he mounted the stairs. 'And don't blame me if you suffer irreparable back damage!'

'Oh, I might blame you for lots of things, reds, but I won't blame you for that.' He laughed and they arrived at her door without him appearing to have broken sweat. Then he finally stood her up and looked down at her.

'OK,' she bristled furiously, 'so you proved that you're a big strong man! Was that the object of the exercise?'

'No,' he answered, leaning against the doorframe as she opened the door. 'Want me to tell you what was?'

They stared at each other and Shannon felt her mouth go suddenly dry because there was no teasing glint in his eye to rescue her from her wild alarm. In fact, his stillness just sent her nervous system into further overdrive.

'No,' she whispered, and he laughed harshly.

'Why? What are you afraid I might say?'

'I really must get to bed now...' she answered desperately.

'And being the perfect gentleman I am,' he said in his deep, caressing voice, 'I wouldn't dream of intruding on your beauty sleep. And being the perfect gentleman that I am, I also wouldn't dream of allowing you to return to Ireland for Christmas with no tales to tell your family of this wonderful city of ours and all it has to offer. So I've decided to take you to my personal favourite jazz club for dinner and an evening of less frenetic fun than you seem to think is necessary for a good time...'

'*You've* decided?' Her body was taking time to recover from its proximity to his. As was her breathing.

'That's right. *I've* decided. Next Saturday. How does that sound?'

'It sounds—'

'Good. I'll pick you up at seven forty-five and don't worry, you'll have a good time.' He leant so that his mouth was almost touching her ear. Her highly sensitised ear. 'Trust me.'

CHAPTER SIX

THE following few days saw a feverish and panicky assault on all the reasonably priced clothes shops in Central London. Shannon couldn't help but marvel at how the cost of clothes, in particular clothes that required the least yardage of fabric, had sneakily crept up almost when she'd had her back turned. One minute she could afford one or two things in Ireland, nothing designer but nothing shabby either, the next minute she was to be found gaping incredulously at price tags that would have brought her bank manager out in a sweat.

What had possessed her to lie? Didn't she know that lying was nothing more than the laying of foundations for future regrets? If she hadn't, then she knew now because she spent most of her waking time regretting her reckless blunder.

It helped on the one hand that Kane was abroad and so couldn't witness her frantic lunchtime forays into increasingly unsuitable shops. On the other hand, his absence gave her ample opportunity to build up feelings of nervous apprehension. When she thought of him carrying her back to her bedsit, his arms engulfing her body, she felt a sick flutter of dismayed panic but then she couldn't understand why because he hadn't touched her, at least not in any way that could have been construed as suggestive.

'Dad phoned last night,' Eleanor said casually, as they were washing dishes on the Friday evening.

'Oh, did he?' Shannon trilled, before clearing her

throat and trying to assume a less sinister tone. 'How is he? Is he having a good time in New York?'

She communicated daily with him by e-mail, but the subjects covered didn't stray from the work arena.

'He's back tomorrow morning,' Eleanor told her brightly. 'He says he's bought me something but he won't say what.'

'Mmm.' Shannon thoughtfully finished washing up and squeezed the sponge of soapy water. In ten minutes Carrie would be coming to take over. 'And have you got anything planned for tomorrow night? Perhaps a special father-daughter bonding thing? Over some chicken nuggets and chips?'

Eleanor gave her one of those looks that implied wisdom beyond her years. *'Father-daughter bonding?'*

'It *does* happen, you know.'

'But Daddy's too...' She spent a few seconds rooting around for an adequate description of her father. 'Too absent-minded when it comes to stuff like that.'

'You two could share a meal,' Shannon persisted, taken with the idea of wriggling out of her unwelcome dinner date, about which she had been reminded only that very morning by e-mail, due to circumstances over which she had no apparent control. 'Carrie will be here with you in the morning. You two could go and do a shop, buy whatever food he likes most, prepare something special...' Her voice trailed off at the wry look being shot at her from the diminutive creature at her side.

'He's taking me to tea,' Eleanor said, 'and, besides, aren't you supposed to be going out with him in the night?'

'Ah, yes!' Shannon forced herself to give a hundred-watt smile. 'Forgot!'

'How could you forget?'

'I just did.' She shrugged as if forgetting dinner dates was an affliction from which she routinely suffered.

'Have you got your little black dress?'

'And how,' Shannon asked curiously, 'did you know that I was wearing a little black dress?' She faced her eight-year-old sparring partner with hands on hips. 'Spill the beans, miss,' she said, waggling one finger at her. 'Or else your pudding days are over!'

Eleanor giggled and looked unthreatened at the prospect.

'Oh, Daddy mentioned it on the phone yesterday. He said that he hoped you hadn't forgotten about your date and that he was dying to see your little black dress. I can't imagine you in a little black dress,' she tacked on undiplomatically, and Shannon only just managed to refrain from agreeing. 'Nor can Dad,' Eleanor continued with ruthless frankness. 'You're always wearing those funny, boring suits.'

'My suits are not funny!' She laughed. 'If they were, they wouldn't be so boring. But you wait until you get into the big, bad world of work. You, too, will find that your wardrobe is limited!'

'What's your dress like?'

'Very small and...well, small is about all there is to say about it.' In fact, it was the smallest dress she had ever owned in her life, but the shop assistant had said it looked great, and on the fifth day of fruitless shopping, with desperation yapping at her ankles, Shannon had cheerfully believed her.

'Is this a work thing, then?' Eleanor asked, dropping her eyes, and so fortunately missing the colour that flooded into Shannon's face.

'That's right! Work-related,' she confirmed. If only.

It was unlikely, however, that an eight-year-old child would understand an invitation that had stemmed from a combination of pity for the poor woman whose knowledge of London was obviously lacking, curiosity to see what she looked like in the small black number which she had somehow made sound wildly exciting and sexy, and sheer devilry at the tacit challenge behind Shannon's inebriated teasing.

'So...not a date...'

'So...not really...'

'Because,' Eleanor said in a rush, 'I wouldn't mind. I mean, it's not as if you're like the last woman Dad brought home for me to meet. She was awful.'

'Hideous, do you mean?' Shannon asked, briefly tussling with her conscience which was telling her not to try and get information out of a child, particularly information that was none of her business, and losing. 'Unappealing? Perhaps spots?'

'Oh, no, Claudia was beautiful, but...you know...'

'Dull?'

'Too clever and full of herself.'

Beautiful, clever and self-confident, Shannon thought with a stab of emotion that felt suspiciously like jealousy. Only a child could have read disadvantages into such a description.

Beautiful, clever and self-confident was not how she felt on Saturday evening at seven-thirty, with fifteen minutes to go. Having decided that she wouldn't get overwhelmed and stupidly dress in her finery with hours to spare, she now found herself frantically putting on her make-up in front of her mirror and anxiously looking at her watch in a race to get herself ready and presentable before Kane rang the doorbell and she had to hurry down to meet him.

The dress, which she had been told made her look sexy, felt like cling film and left so little to the imagination that she couldn't fathom why she'd been persuaded to buy the thing in the first place. Ten minutes of temporary insanity and here she was, stuffed into sausage skin with far too much leg showing for comfort. The neckline was modest enough but, then, Shannon thought, inspecting herself in the small mirror on the wardrobe door, it would have to be if only to compensate for the plunging back that made wearing a bra out of the question.

Thank goodness it was winter and she could hide behind her thick coat at least for the duration of the drive to the club.

The red hair at least didn't seem too overpowering. She'd had it trimmed into a bob a few days earlier and it swung nicely around her face, if with somewhat glaring intensity. There was nothing that could be done about that. She experimentally swung her head from side to side and was quite pleased with how it looked. Better than tied back into something puerile and unattractive which was how she normally wore it.

It will be a subdued evening during which I shall try very hard not to gabble. I will refuse all drink on some pretext or other and will act like a mature and sophisticated woman instead of an eccentric, unpredictable one.

By the time her bell buzzed from the downstairs front door, Shannon was ready to face Kane. She took her time slipping on her coat and gloves and greeted him five minutes later with a controlled smile.

'You've done something with your hair' were his opening words, which sent a little rush of pleasure through her. He was lounging against the doorway in his black coat, with a cream silk scarf draped casually around his neck.

'I've had it trimmed.' She tossed her head back in the manner of a film star. 'Do you like it?'

'It's very nice,' he said. 'Very chic.'

In the darkness, Shannon looked at him narrowly, wondering whether there was some hidden meaning in his remark to which she should take immediate offence, but the contours of his face were bland, and there was nothing remotely smug in his voice as he began talking about his trip to New York.

'Have you ever been to New York?' he asked, as he manipulated the car smoothly along back roads she wouldn't have recognised in a thousand years.

It crossed her mind that it would have been glorious to have swapped notes on life in the Big Apple. Unfortunately some lies just couldn't be countenanced.

'You could rephrase that,' Shannon said tartly, 'to "Have you ever been anywhere except London and Ireland?"'

'You've *never* been anywhere else?'

'I know. Shocking, isn't it? I've never even been on a plane! Just one of the many things I never seemed to get around to doing!'

'Now you sound very brittle and you're not a brittle person, are you? How have you managed to live your life without setting foot on a plane in this day and age of cheap air travel?'

Shannon chewed her lip, wondering whether she should counter his kind curiosity with something trivial and vague, but in the end she said thoughtfully, 'I guess that, growing up, there was never the money to go around. Don't forget how many of us there were, and Mum would never have taken a few on holiday and left the rest behind. So we went on holidays to the beach, camping, to the countryside. And by the time I started working, well, I never seemed to have any lump sums of money around that I could use for a holiday somewhere hot.'

'You must have saved something from working,' he persisted wryly, 'if you lived at home with your family and had no astronomical rent to pay. Or did you spend it all on clothes? Warn me now so that I have an idea of what to expect when Eleanor gets older and insists on augmenting her pocket money with a weekend job! Tell me she won't blow the lot on shopping!' He flicked an amused sideways glance at her then looked back ahead of him, his mouth curved into a slight smile.

Why did he group her and his daughter together? It was ridiculous. Shannon suddenly felt perversely pleased that she'd worn the skin-tight number after all.

'Actually, I usually ended up buying stuff for my younger brothers,' Shannon said reluctantly. Of course she had bought clothes for herself and gone out with her friends, but she had also paid rent to her mother and it was true that pay days had always been a source of treats for the kids. It had always seemed natural to share.

'That's great,' Kane said warmly, and she grimaced.

'I don't suppose Eleanor will run into that particular problem,' she pointed out. She'd just succeeded, she thought wryly, in making herself sound like a prosaic goody two-shoes! 'She'll probably blow all her money on clothes and shoes and holidays and will leave poor old Dad picking up the tab!'

'Maybe.' Kane turned around in his seat to manoeuvre the car into a parking space, his arm splayed along the back of her seat behind the headrest. 'But then again, maybe,' he said, facing her but with his arm still behind her seat, 'she'll grow up with other siblings and shed out all her money on treats for them. Who knows?'

'You mean you want another family?' For some reason, the thought was shocking. It also made her wonder, uncomfortably, whether there was another woman on the scene somewhere. A prospective Ms Right, discreetly lurking in the background. Very discreetly, since she had seen nothing of her, but, then, Kane Lindley was a very discreet man, wasn't he? If he wanted to hide something, he would do it with the utmost tact.

'Not,' she added hastily, 'that it's any of my business.'

'You sound astounded. Isn't the desire to procreate as natural as breathing?'

They walked into the jazz club which was small, intimate and reassuringly dark so that he couldn't see the flush that had spread across her cheekbones.

'Your coat?' He reached to help her out of it and Shannon resisted the urge to cling tightly to the comforting barrier of wool concealing her scantily clad body.

'I might be cold.'

'I doubt it. It's pretty warm in here and after a couple of dances you'll be hot.'

'A couple of dances?'

'If you can slow your tempo to accommodate an old man.'

'I wish you'd stop referring to yourself as an old man,' she grumbled, relinquishing her coat with reluctance and refusing to wilt under his thorough inspection. 'You certainly didn't seem old when…when you…'

'Swept you off your feet? Well, thank you very kindly. I trust that was a compliment?' He glanced down at her, very slowly.

'The little black dress,' he murmured. 'It *is* little, isn't it? I hope the men here can stand the strain on their blood pressure.'

Her own blood pressure appeared to be soaring through the roof as he continued to gaze at her with her coat draped elegantly over his arm.

'Do you know,' he said with a low laugh, 'I didn't quite believe you when you told me that you possessed a little black number?'

Shannon gave a tinkling laugh. Tinkling and, she hoped, mildly amused at the suggestion herself. 'Didn't you? I have a wardrobe of them back in Ireland!'

'Have you now?' They handed their coats to the girl at the counter and were given a disc which Kane slipped into the pocket of his jacket.

'Oh, yes. Of course, I couldn't bring them all down here to London. I knew I wouldn't have the space to hang them.'

'What a complex little creature you are, reds,' he said, as they were shown to their table which was tucked away at the side. Very cosy, very intimate, very nerve-racking. 'How to equate the girl who spent her hard-earned money buying presents for her siblings with a provocative woman with a wardrobe of daring numbers?' He called a waitress over and ordered a bottle of champagne and then resumed his inspection of her. 'Perhaps I'm a typical man who naturally puts women into categories, and the category of someone who's obviously so good with children doesn't seem to slip into the category of a woman who willingly flaunts her charms by night.'

Flaunts her charms? Well, on the one hand, he *was*, she thought with heady pleasure, admitting that she had charms to flaunt. On the other hand, the woman he was describing didn't seem to bear any relation to her at all.

'That *is* a typical man,' she agreed in a smoky voice.

In the presence of this man, she was discovering another side of her which hadn't existed before. Someone sensual and responsive, far more sensual and responsive, in fact, than she had ever felt in the company of Eric Gallway, whose pursuit had made her feel giddy enough, but giddy in the manner of a teenager. She'd enjoyed his attention, but most of all she'd enjoyed the sensation of feeling herself to be in love. Well, she wasn't in love now, but Kane certainly had the knack of making her feel like a woman.

Perhaps, at long last, she was finally breaking out of her chrysalis to spread her wings and fly free from the cheerful girl next door she had always been. Just the thought of this new woman emerging sent a racy thrill through her body.

At the back of her mind, she recalled that she *was* his secretary, but the boundary lines were blurred, particularly as she saw him so regularly out of work, even if it was still in the controlled setting of his house with his daughter present.

'Or maybe,' she mused thoughtfully, 'you've always mixed with women who slotted into one role or the other. Beautiful career-women, for example, clever and self-confident but unable to cross the barriers into normal, boisterous family life...?'

'Maybe I have...' He sipped his champagne and continued to look at her over the rim of the glass. 'So do you think I've been playing it all wrong?'

'I think so!' Shannon said airily. Funny stuff, champagne. It felt as though she wasn't drinking at all.

'What do you think I should do to correct my preconceptions?' he asked meekly.

'Look beneath the surface.' Shannon gave him a wise look from under her mascara-tipped lashes.

'I'll try my best,' he replied gravely.

There was a sudden flurry of activity on the slightly raised circular platform towards the back of the room and then the jazz band appeared, eight men dressed in black who then proceeded to give a spirited rendition of a recognisable Gershwin piece, which was heartily applauded, followed by a more subdued and atmospheric number which saw couples flocking to the dance floor.

Shannon turned to show her appreciation of the music to Kane just as a tall, dark-haired beauty materialised at his side and tapped him on his shoulder.

She leant over him so that her long raven hair rippled along the back of his shirt, exposing in the process, Shannon noticed viciously, a bird's-eye view of a very ample cleavage. She could feel her heart beat savagely inside her and gulped down some of the champagne so quickly that she had to stifle an undignified coughing fit. She couldn't hear what was being said but she had no need to be an expert lip-reader to see, from the body language of the slender arm casually resting along Kane's shoulder, that they were more than just passing acquaintances.

'Would you mind,' the woman said, leaning over Kane to address Shannon, so that the generous breasts which seemed intent on bursting forth from the tight-fitting red top rested tantalisingly close to his face, 'if I drag this gorgeous beast up for a dance?'

'Be my guest,' Shannon responded through tightly clenched teeth, thinking that she could drag the gorgeous beast backwards through a holly bush for all she cared, but Kane was having none of it. He made his apologies with a rueful smile and a shrug of his broad shoulders and the woman departed with a 'Maybe later' promise between them.

'My apologies for not introducing you,' Kane said, standing up and extending his hand for Shannon's so that she had no option but to ungracefully submit to a dance, 'but the music was a bit loud and I didn't want to keep Carole from her dinner companion...' Another slow, soulful jazz number was being played, and he pulled her close to him, cupping the small of her back with one hand while the other clasped her own hand which felt ridiculously small engulfed in his.

'She didn't seem all that bothered to keep her dinner companion waiting,' Shannon pointed out coolly. Her cheek was resting lightly against his chest and she could feel his heart beating.

'Well, perhaps I thought it rude to keep *my* dinner companion waiting,' he said into her hair, and Shannon drew away slightly to look at him.

'It didn't bother me one way or another.'

'Didn't it?'

Her green eyes were unable to sustain the glitter of his dark ones and she was the first to look away. It was impossible not to feel vulnerable and disadvantaged, she thought, when she had to crane her neck upwards to look at him, like a woman arching up to receive her lover's kiss.

'No.' Shannon's voice was resolute. 'I was more than happy to sit on my own and listen to the music.'

'I wouldn't dream of letting you do any such thing.'

'Because you're too much of a gentleman?' she heard herself sniping, and he smiled.

'Possibly.'

His ambiguous reply sent a flare of dangerous excitement coursing through her body which was instantly quenched by the memory of the glamorous brunette who, from all appearances, would have ditched her dinner companion for the sake of an evening with Kane.

'So,' she asked after a short silence, during which his body against hers seemed to burn with increasing heat, 'who *is* she, anyway? Feel free not to answer if you don't consider it any of my business.' Her voice implied that whether he chose to answer or not was a matter of supreme indifference to her because she was merely making convenient small talk.

He pulled her fractionally closer to him so that their bodies were now grinding against one another, as though engaged in a slow mating ritual. Shannon shivered.

'She *was* a business acquaintance and...personal friend...'

'*Was* a personal friend?' Shannon asked innocently. 'Oh, dear. Friendships are so valuable. Did you fall out?'

This time it was his turn to draw back and look down at her, catching her wide green gaze with enough of a dry smile to make her very aware that he knew what she was playing at.

'We concluded our relationship,' he said. 'And if you want to find out precisely what kind of relationship we had, why don't you just ask?'

Shannon flushed and stared at the button on his shirt for a few seconds. When she was sure that her expression was composed, she looked back up at him and smiled sweetly. 'I take it that it was an intimate relationship and I assure you I'm not in the least interested in prying for details.'

'Shall I give them to you anyway? To satisfy whatever faint shreds of curiosity there might be playing around in sweet little head of yours?'

'If you like.'

'I met her through work. She's a lawyer, and we got

to know one another earlier this year over a period of a few months, but time showed that we weren't suited at all and we mutually agreed to call it a day.'

'*She* looked as though she might be persuaded to re-kindle the affair,' Shannon said, feeling horrible because the remark was so obviously catty, but he didn't appear to take any offence.

'Possibly. But...' He tucked her hair behind one delicate ear and whispered, 'Once I've decided on something, I don't change my mind.' Which was just the sort of remark to egg on her already seething curiosity to further unprepossessing heights. Fortunately, before she could launch into yet more questions, the number ended and she used the brief respite in the music to mention food.

And for the next hour they chatted about non-threatening topics. Safe discussions about music and Ireland and celebrities and Kane's massive experience of other countries, while Shannon's champagne-fuddled brain tried to pinpoint precise things he had said to her while they had been dancing. The brunette did not reappear, although halfway through their *crème brûlée* Shannon spotted her on the dance floor in the arms of a tall, attractive, fair-haired man who seemed to be having a whale of a time, his hands roaming over every inch of her body within respectable limits.

'Having a good time?' Kane leaned towards her and Shannon gave a merry laugh.

'Fabulous food...great music... Of course I am!' More than that, she felt wonderfully alive, burning with energy, in fact.

'In that case, care for another dance?'

'I need one,' she said breathlessly, 'if only to burn off some of the calories of the food I've just eaten!'

'Nonsense, you don't need to lose an ounce of weight.'

'You haven't seen me…seen me without…' The observation, which had started off impulsively enough, trailed off into an embarrassed silence.

'No, but I've felt you.' He rescued her from the no-entry road down which her conversational impulse had foolishly taken her.

'You've *what*?'

'Felt the shape of your body through that very minute dress you're wearing, and believe me when I tell you that you don't need to watch what you eat.'

Shannon narrowed her eyes at the open, innocent expression on his face. 'Well, it doesn't matter how much I eat, I'll never attain the proportions of the lovely Carole,' she said nastily, falling into step with him once again and feeling as though their bodies were in perfect sync.

'She is rather tall and well-endowed, isn't she?' he said with a low laugh that brushed against her cheek like warm breath.

'And clever with it,' she couldn't resist adding.

'And very clever with it,' Kane concurred. 'Just the sort of woman I should be steering well clear of, in fact. Too one-dimensional.' He gave another low laugh which made Shannon wonder whether he was being condescending at her expense but her suspicious eyes met another of those bland, innocent looks with which it was difficult to find fault.

'Eleanor didn't care for her anyway,' he added, which gave Shannon a treacherous stab of satisfaction. 'And I'm old-fashioned enough to want approval from my daughter for any woman I choose to have a serious relationship with.'

'That's not old-fashioned, it's considerate and compassionate. I know my mother would never have contemplated settling down with a man who didn't get full approval from all of us.'

'A tall order for any man,' Kane said with a groan, and Shannon giggled.

'I know. Not that we wouldn't want our mum to have every chance of happiness...'

'But to appeal to seven! I take it your mother never remarried?'

Shannon shook her head. 'She's had quite a few dates. She's still an attractive woman considering we should all have put a thousand lines on her face over the years, but she's always said that her hands were too full to contemplate settling down and adding a man to the list of people to take care of.'

'Worries about you all, does she?' He unclasped one hand to place it at the back of her neck so that her hair fell over his fingers. She could feel every touch of every individual finger like a branding iron against her flesh. Thank goodness he was unaware of her reaction, she thought jerkily, because he would laugh his head off if he knew. In fact, in the cold light of morning and without the effects of champagne drifting like incense in her brain, she would, no doubt, laugh her head off at the memory herself.

'Of course she does,' she said. 'Don't all mothers? No, that was naïve of me. Of course they don't all. We were lucky with Mum and I guess we sometimes take that for granted. But *you* worry about Eleanor, don't you?'

'Oh, inordinately. As you say, it should come with the territory.'

They danced in silence for a while and in fact, the

snippet of conversation lay semi-forgotten at the back of Shannon's mind when, on the way back to her flat, he raised it once again via the circuitous route of quizzing her more about her family. If he seemed suddenly fascinated by her background, Shannon didn't notice. The champagne had taken its toll and she was on the verge of falling asleep, even though she kept forcing herself to open her eyes every time she felt herself beginning to drift off. She had a vision of herself slumbering peacefully against the door of his car, blissfully unaware of everything, mouth half-open, and it didn't make a pretty picture.

But she could barely answer his questions without yawning, so when he slipped his vital question in, she was almost unaware of the implications. She assumed it was yet another family-type question until her brain deciphered his message and she sat up abruptly and asked him to repeat what he had just said.

'I merely said,' he obliged, talking very slowly and keeping his eyes fixed to the road ahead, 'that you should consider leaving that hovel you're renting in view of the anguish it would cause your mother, if nothing else, and move in with me.'

'*Move in with you.*' It was such a ludicrous suggestion that Shannon nearly burst into laughter at the thought of it. 'Are you crazy? What sort of offer is that?'

'A perfectly reasonable one, as it happens.' He slowed down as they approached her building and managed to find a space for his car directly outside, but when she turned to open the car door, he swiftly reached across and stopped her by placing his hand over hers.

'*Reasonable?*' Shannon shrieked.

'Just listen to me for a minute.' He let go of her hand and sat back with one arm resting loosely on the steering-wheel. 'That bedsit of yours is no place to live. In fact, your landlord should be shot for carving up the house into such small rooms just to squeeze more money out of gullible young people...'

'I am not gullible!'

'And as you agreed earlier on, your mother would hit the roof if she knew your living conditions...'

'Well, she doesn't!'

'So what better solution than for you to move in with me? My house is more than big enough to accommodate an extra person. In fact, you'll have a suite so that your privacy won't be invaded in any way whatsoever, and it would ease my mind if I knew you didn't have to endure that walk back to this dump every evening. Naturally your working hours with regard to Eleanor would remain unchanged, and if you wanted to go out in the evenings, Carrie would babysit as she always has in the past...'

Shannon felt as though she had been cruising blithely along only to suddenly find herself on a mad roller-coaster ride.

'No, wait just a minute—'

'Of course, the situation would only stand until you find somewhere else, and as I won't charge you any rent, you would be able to save all the more quickly for just that...'

'No, it really is out of the—'

'Think about it overnight.' Kane stepped out of the car and opened her door for her. She nearly fell out.

'We'll discuss it,' he continued implacably, 'first thing on Monday morning.'

And before she could utter another word of protest, he was back in his car, patiently waiting to make sure she was safely inside before driving away.

CHAPTER SEVEN

NO WONDER Kane hadn't offered to see her up to her door, make sure she travelled the two flights of stairs without being accosted five times on the way, checked under the sofa for possible snakes. Discretion had overcome valour! He must have known, Shannon fumed, that she would have clobbered him over the head with something very large and very hard!

She'd never heard such a ridiculous suggestion in her whole life and she knew why he'd made it. Because life would be infinitely easier for him if he had her in place as nanny and his over-developed protective instincts would be satisfied, knowing that she didn't have to scurry like a fugitive along the dark streets leading to her flat every time she left his house.

Did he really imagine that she would relinquish her freedom and be grateful for the opportunity?

Her bedsit might be the last word in undesirable, but it was hers and she had no one looking over her shoulder every time she sneezed!

Shannon tried to imagine life under Kane Lindley's roof but when she did her mind was overwhelmed by suffocating thoughts of never being able to escape him. It was bad enough trying not to be aware of his presence when she was at his house with Eleanor for three hours after work. It was bad enough constantly crossing that line between secretary and babysitter, without having to endure it twenty-four hours a day! Never mind his logic about saving up to rent somewhere halfway decent!

Logic, she thought sourly, might rule his life, but it certainly didn't rule hers!

'It's a very thoughtful offer,' Sandy told her treacherously the next day over lunch. 'London's not safe at night. I mean, don't you feel worried having to walk back to your flat in that part of town?'

'You're supposed to take my side, Sandy,' Shannon complained, toying with the pasta on her plate.

'You could always share a house, like me. It means I can afford a room in a much nicer area...'

'And have four people breathing down your neck! I need my privacy!' Sandy shared a large house on the outskirts of Hampstead with four other girls, and whenever Shannon was around, there always seemed to be people bursting through doors or having loud telephone conversations in the room next door, or else opening fridge doors and speculating on who had stolen their food. Sandy might enjoy the constant hum of activity but Shannon suspected that it would drive her crazy.

'Well, he said you would have all the privacy you wanted...'

'And pigs might fly. What's this?' She stabbed a peculiar object in her plate of pasta and held it up for examination.

'Oh, Alfredo had one or two scallops going spare so I flung them in.'

'It's a strange addition, don't you think?'

'Not for anyone with refined tastebuds. Anyway, you're changing the subject. If his house is that big, you won't even have to see him at all.' There was a sudden flurry of activity as the kitchen was invaded by several people who all seemed to be hunting out scraps for lunch, stopping to chat *en route* and dip into what was on offer in the dish in the middle of the table. Having a conversation was impossible in Sandy's house.

'And as he pointed out,' Sandy continued, oblivious to the chaos, 'you'll be able to save lots of money and put a deposit on somewhere a bit more upmarket. In fact, you'd probably only have to stay there for a couple of months and your finances would be sorted out. Stop playing with that food and eat up. You'll fade away to nothing.'

No help from that quarter, Shannon thought, but after delivering a long lecture on the role of friends who should always support one another and not try to introduce counter-arguments which only clouded the issue, she allowed herself to be diverted into their usual gossipy chat about what was happening to whom and why.

After all her weekend seething and fulminating, it was almost an anticlimax to get into work the following day, only to discover that Kane had been called away on urgent business and wouldn't see her until possibly later that evening, if not the following morning. No mention of what they had spoken about on Saturday night, and she wondered whether he had forgotten the whole thing already. Maybe at the time he'd been roaring drunk even though he'd seemed as sober as a judge. Perhaps he just hid it well and was, in fact, one of those people who seemed to suffer no effects from alcohol except inexplicable memory loss the following day.

The thought cheered her up. By five o'clock she had come to the comforting conclusion, having spoken to him twice on the telephone during which he had mentioned nothing of what had been said, that he had decided to drop the whole issue. He had probably sensed that under that open, cheerful and seemingly malleable exterior there beat a heart of steel.

Or maybe, she thought to herself, he, too, had realised the implications of his offer. That he would see more of her than he might find palatable. Judging from the beauty at the jazz club, he had a life of his own to pursue and maybe he had reached the conclusion that one Irish girl with a tendency to be too outspoken for her own good might just be a fly in his ointment.

She was due to be at his house to supervise Eleanor by five-thirty but it was nearly six by the time she arrived, to find Kane's car sprawled on the driveway. Before she could ring the bell, the door was open and he was standing in front of her, dressed casually in a pair of cords and a rugby-style sweatshirt that made her hurriedly avert her eyes. Too much masculinity at too close a range.

'I thought you said you were away on urgent business,' she greeted him, as he stood aside to let her enter.

'One thing I admire about you,' he reflected drily, shutting the front door, 'is your talent for bypassing social niceties.'

'Well, I didn't expect to find you here,' Shannon told him by way of apology. 'You said you'd be away until tomorrow morning.'

'I said I *might*.'

'Where's Eleanor?' She tried to peer past him but failed.

'Actually, spending a night with her friend.'

Shannon looked at his coldly. 'In which case, why didn't you inform me?'

Kane, infuriatingly, grinned. 'You're very cute when you try to be cutting. Perhaps because it's so out of character.'

Trust him to leave her speechless. She recovered quickly. 'I won't be needed in that case.'

'Now, whatever gives you that idea?'

Lost for words twice in the space of as many seconds, Shannon contented herself by glaring icily, and he relented with a mock gesture of surrender.

'OK. You're still needed...' he let the words linger tantalisingly in the silence between them '...because I have a visitor to see you. Waiting in the kitchen, as a matter of fact.' He strode off, leaving her to hurriedly get out of her coat and trip along behind him while she frantically tried to work out who this so-called visitor was. Only a handful of people knew where she lived.

'What visitor?' she managed to hiss before they reached the kitchen, and he stopped so abruptly to face her that she nearly staggered into his chest.

'No introductions will be needed. That's all I'll say. Wouldn't want to spoil the surprise.'

He stood dramatically aside for her to precede him and then waited behind as Shannon walked into the kitchen and her visitor stood up with arms outstretched.

'Mum! What are you doing here?' She was aware of Kane standing behind her and she didn't have to look at his face to know that he was the arch-manipulator behind her mother's sudden appearance on the scene. Arch-manipulator with a specific purpose in mind, and the purpose, she suspected wildly, had nothing to do with a tender reunion of mother and daughter for a cup of tea and a cosy chat.

By way of response, her mother engulfed her in a hug, then stood back and inspected her from arm's length.

'Shannon, you've lost weight.'

Her mother was a slender woman with short brown hair and a habit of looking ferocious when she chose. Right now she was looking ferociously at her daughter and Shannon quailed and stammered out something inarticulate by way of denial.

'Don't you try and tell me I'm wrong,' her mother countered with a voice that precluded any further debate on the subject. 'You've lost weight and your lovely gentleman friend had every right to be concerned.' She gave the lovely gentleman friend a warm conspirational look and Shannon controlled the insane impulse to spin around and sock him on his gloating jaw.

'He's not *my lovely gentleman friend*, Mum. He's my employer and *he has no reason to be concerned about me*. I *have* told him that,' she said in a voice laced with the promise of retribution, 'so *I hope he hasn't made the mistake of fetching you all the way from Ireland over nothing!*'

'I don't think my baby's welfare is *nothing*,' her mother said reprovingly, so that Shannon wanted to groan. 'You led me to believe that everything was a bed of roses down here, Shannon. I thank my good Lord that this young man of yours had the sense to call me up and let me know one or two facts!'

'He's not *my young man*.'

The young man in question finally saw fit to sidle past Shannon into the kitchen and offer her a cup of coffee.

'Or something stronger, although it *is* a little on the early side for wine...'

'Oh, my Shannon doesn't drink. A good, strong cup of tea for the both of us would be a delight. Then we can have a nice little chat about things.'

'Very sensible,' Kane agreed, ignoring the killing look that Shannon directed at him.

'Things?' Shannon said weakly. 'What things?'

'Why don't you two ladies go to the sitting room and I'll bring the tea through?' Kane said, giving her a soothing smile that made her want to breathe fire. 'And some of those lovely home-made shortbread biscuits you brought with you, Rose.'

Rose? *Rose?* So now he and her mother were on first-name terms? She watched aghast as her mother gave him another warm smile, the warm smile of someone who had fallen victim to Kane Lindley's charm. Shannon felt herself hustled out of the kitchen by her mother tugging her along and only had a fleeting opportunity to glance backwards over her shoulder at Kane who was busying himself with a tin on the counter, presumably home of the lovely shortbread biscuits.

'What a beautiful house, wouldn't you agree?' Rose said, looking approvingly around her as they passed through the hall and into the sitting room. 'Kane gave me a guided tour of the house and I must say it's beautiful. So quiet in the midst of all this noise and pollution. A haven, if that's the word I'm looking for.'

'He gave you a *guided tour*? How long have you been here, Mum?'

'Oh since around eleven-thirty this morning, darling. You *really do* look gaunt, Shannon. You haven't been eating properly, have you? And I thought you were old enough to look after yourself down here. I should have known better! Didn't I tell you that it would be a mistake, coming here to London? On your own? Away from your family?' She was shaking her head as she said this and Shannon felt as though various lifelines were slipping away, out of her grasp, leaving her defenceless and gasping for air.

'Mum…'

'Now, don't you ''Mum'' me, Shannon.' She sat down and primly folded her hands on her lap.

'Kane had no right to get in touch with you.'

'He had every right, my girl. It's a blessing that there's someone in this godless city who cares about your welfare. He explained how worried he was at the state of your living quarters—'

'My living quarters are fine, Mum!' Shannon protested feebly. 'Adequate, at any rate.'

'Well, my girl, I'll be the judge of that. Kane suggested that the best thing might be if I go with you to have a look for myself.'

Shannon's last remaining wall of defence crumbled in the face of the implacable steamroller now looking at her, and there was a minute of respectful silence while she contemplated the outcome of any such impending visit to her bedsit. There was no opportunity to vent her fury at the instigator of it all until much later that night, after her mother had been ensconced in a bed in one of the guest rooms.

'You...you...*rat*!' Shannon spluttered, stamping into the kitchen to confront a cool, calm and collected Kane who had managed to spend the evening further ingratiating himself into her mother's good books by saying all the right things, making all the right noises and behaving in the sort of gallant manner calculated to overcome all maternal obstacles.

'Coffee? Nightcap?'

'Don't you *coffee* and *nightcap* me!' She looked at him with withering rage. 'How *dare* you bring my poor mother all the way here just to suit yourself?'

'Sit down. You look as though you're about to explode,' he said with his vast mastery of understatement. He indicated a chair at the kitchen table facing him and Shannon flung herself into it, making choked noises under her breath.

'Now, why don't you get a grip and we can discuss

this like two adults?' He was drinking a glass of port and appeared utterly serene in the face of her blistering gaze. 'Sure you won't join me in a glass of port? My little teetotaller? Tut, tut, tut, fancy letting your mother think that you hated the demon drink...'

'I'll join you in a glass of port,' Shannon informed him through gritted teeth, 'if you'll allow me to pour it over that conniving head of yours.'

He shook his head and poured her a glass. 'Now you're being childish. You have to admit that your mother saw my point of view completely, and aren't you happy that she felt confident about giving you her blessing to shelter under my roof until you found somewhere more respectable to live? I told her all about Eleanor, of course, and she was delighted to think that you would be joining in a family instead of living on your own.'

'My life is none of your business! You had no right—'

'You don't want to accept help, but accepting help sometimes can show strength of character. If you're nervous about sharing my house...'

'Nervous? Why on earth should I be nervous?'

'I don't know. Perhaps you think that things might be different somehow if you moved in. Less of an employer-employee situation...'

'I don't think anything of the sort,' Shannon told him frigidly, distracted from her argument by his sweeping assumption that his presence might affect her somehow. Did he imagine that at closer quarters she might develop an unlikely crush?

'Then what's the problem with accepting a helping hand for a month or two until you find somewhere else? Your freedom won't in any way be curtailed. I'm not going to take advantage of your good nature...' He paused and stroked his chin reflectively. 'Well, perhaps good nature is a bit strong,' he murmured slyly. 'Put it this way, you can come and go as you please.'

'How did you manage to persuade my mother to come here? How did you know where she lived?'

'Your next of kin on your personnel file in answer to question two. And in answer to question one, I simply appealed to her good sense to come and see how you were.'

'Ugh. Sickening.' She knew that she would get precisely nowhere if she continued ranting and railing. Her mother had been pathetic enough over Mrs Porter's superbly prepared dinner, treating Kane as though he was the impersonation of everything wonderful and even having the cheek to slide her the odd glance or two indicating how much she approved of him.

Her mother, who had always been a dragon of embarrassing, inquisitive questions when it came to her boyfriends, had melted in the face of Kane's studied thoughtfulness. She had treated Shannon's stuttering, wrath-filled protests over the washing-up with incomprehension, pointing out that she should be grateful to have found such a considerate employer who was responsible enough to take an interest in her well-being. After half an hour of this, Shannon had felt like flinging herself over the edge of the nearest precipice.

'Your mother didn't seem to think I was sickening.'

Shannon eyed him narrowly. 'She's probably suffering from undiagnosed senile dementia.'

'In fact, she thought I was a very responsible, thoughtful kind of guy...as she herself said on several occasions if my memory serves me right...'

Shannon wondered how she was ever going to spend even a week in the company of someone who had a tendency to get under her skin like a worrisome burr without going mad. But move in she would because she had been left no option.

Her mother had been predictably appalled at the bedsit, peering at everything, checking her fridge, clucking her tongue, shaking her head and generally acting as though the mere fact that her beloved daughter had lived in such a place without informing her constituted a mortal sin. She had implied to her trailing daughter that she had somehow been rescued by her saintly employer from a vicious fate of assault at knifepoint and had then proceeded to deliver a scathing lecture on her poor eating habits. As though the loss of a few pounds were somehow inextricably linked to her living arrangements.

'Well, if I move in here—'

'When, you mean.'

'I intend to lay down a few ground rules,' she continued, ignoring Kane's smug interruption. 'First of all, I don't work as an out-of-hours secretary if you have anything that needs typing. Secondly, I don't want anyone looking over my shoulder at what I'm doing—'

'Will you be doing anything that might tempt me to do that?' he asked mildly.

'And, thirdly, I don't intend to clock in and out and ask permission to breathe. Oh, and, fourthly, I have to give you some rent money.'

'Absolutely no rent money,' he said forbiddingly.

'I don't like the idea of accepting favours,' Shannon informed him stiffly.

'Why ever not? Sometimes it's important to see the big picture or else we end up missing valuable opportunities by getting entangled in the little things. One of the most important pieces of advice I can give you is to have long-term vision.'

'I didn't realise that I had asked for any important pieces of advice.'

'I wouldn't be here today if I hadn't accepted a few favours along the way.'

Shannon looked at him suspiciously. 'I can't imagine *you* accepting favours from anyone,' she muttered.

'Hmm. For a confirmed non-drinker, I must say you've managed to finish that glass of port in record time. Can I pour you another?' Kane shot her a grin that was wickedly amused. 'Didn't you drink at all when you lived in Ireland?'

'Of course I did! I just didn't…drink in the house.'

'And what other little secrets have you been keeping from that delightful mother of yours?'

Shannon thought that she might hit him at any moment.

'I mean, does she know about the wild and irresponsible life you've been leading down here?'

'I haven't been leading a wild and irresponsible life!' She had nightmarish visions of her mother quizzing her on her after-work activities, making dubious leaps of the imagination and coming to the wrong conclusions. 'And stop interfering,' she added as an afterthought.

'You're right.' He stood up and flexed his muscles. 'I'm nothing but an interfering old busybody.' His smile was a devastating mix of rueful apology and old-fashioned charm.

Did he expect her to buy that nonsense? she wondered. His words implied that he was nothing but a harmless senior citizen whose nosy interference she should indulge, if only to humour him. Ha! His self-effacing description couldn't have been further from the truth, as they both very well knew.

'True,' Shannon said sweetly in agreement. 'And I

personally can't think of anything worse than an interfering old busybody.'

Kane didn't care for that. She could tell from his frowning expression, and her saccharine smile grew broader.

'I suppose,' she mused, 'when a person gets old there's very little left to amuse them but interfering in other people's lives. They bustle about, poking and prying, and don't even realise how irritating they are.'

'You have a point,' Kane conceded. But before she could rest on her temporary victory and enjoy the taste of it before it evaporated altogether, he added, *sotto voce*, 'Next time I see Rose I must ask her whether she ever considered me an interfering old fool with nothing better to do.' He laughed softly to himself, as if remembering a particularly pleasant thought. 'Perhaps she might see it as her duty to try and patch up my poor, wounded ego.'

While Shannon was trying to find a suitably cutting retort to this, he sauntered towards the kitchen door and paused, to throw over his shoulder, 'Oh, forgot to mention. I told your mum that you'd take a couple of days off work to move and show her around a bit. And before you thank me, there's absolutely no need.' Then he was gone before she could launch a few well-deserved verbal missiles in his direction.

'I don't know how you could let yourself be conned into believing Kane Lindley,' Shannon grumbled to her mother two days later in the airport lounge, where they were waiting for Rose's flight to be called. Trust him to finish her mother's trip with flourish. First-class air fare back to Ireland. Excessive and flamboyant, she thought to herself, although when she'd tried to share this humble opinion with her mother, she'd immediately found herself in the dubious role of small-minded daughter suffering a bad attack of sour grapes just because she hadn't got her own way.

'Now, don't be silly, Shannon. I wasn't conned into anything. Kane has chosen to take you under his wing and I must say I have utmost trust in him.'

'Why?' Shannon cried. 'Why?'

'Because he's a dying breed, my girl. A true gentleman.'

'When it suits him.'

'And Eleanor is a charming little girl. I can see how fond she is of you.' Her mother smiled warmly at her daughter. 'You always did have a gift with the little ones. It'll do you the world of good, living there for a little while, give you time to eat properly, get your money together for somewhere better to live.'

'Just so long as you don't go into a state of shock when I tell you that I'm moving out,' Shannon warned. 'And you might as well know that I'll never be able to rent anywhere like Kane's house. I'll still only be able to afford somewhere small.'

'Small doesn't have to be dangerous and dingy.'

Her mother. Brainwashed. It was enough to make a girl ill. But Shannon had to admit, as the days rolled by, that Kane was true to his word. Carrie still collected Eleanor from school, and on the very first evening had asked Shannon to let her know what nights she planned to be away so that she could come over to babysit. There would be no question of her being trapped in a full-time nanny role.

Neither had she found herself obliged to politely accept lifts to work with Kane in the mornings. He left before seven, giving her an hour to get herself together before having to leave the house. And at the office he was utterly professional. However long the situation lasted, there would be no intrusion into her personal space.

Amidst the general upheaval, she had almost forgotten about the Christmas play until Eleanor reminded her one morning before she was about to leave for school.

'I hope you haven't forgotten about this afternoon' were her opening words as she went into the office to find Kane sitting at her desk and riffling through her in tray.

'Have you seen that Jones file? I'm sure I had it on my desk before I left work yesterday.'

'Have you checked your briefcase?'

'Good point.' He abandoned the abortive search and focused on her. 'What about this afternoon?'

'Eleanor's play?'

'Damn. Damn, damn, damn.'

'I'm afraid she'll be terribly disappointed if you don't turn up,' Shannon told him quietly. 'I specifically arranged no meetings for you this afternoon after one-thirty and that meeting shouldn't overrun. I have to tell you that I'm really disappointed. I just can't believe that you could have forgotten about it. She's shown us her routine often enough, for Pete's sake!' As soon as the words were out she realised how cosily domesticated they made them both seem. Like a traditional couple playing at happy families instead of a boss and his secretary who had found herself in the unnatural situation of living under his roof.

To hide her burning cheeks, she began flapping around the coat rail, then spent a few seconds busying herself by dusting down her coat, as though it had somehow accumulated grit on the journey to work. When she turned to face him, she was less flushed.

'Joke,' Kane said, standing up and spinning her chair round to face her but keeping both his hands on the back of it.

'What?'

'Joke. Of course I remembered about the play. A few months ago I may have forgotten about it, but I've come a long way since those days of absentee father.' He waited until she had primly positioned herself on the chair before swivelling it round to face him and leaning over her with his hands on either side of the chair. 'Now I find our domestic little routines quite appealing, just as you seem to.'

Shannon was beginning to feel faint at his closeness. 'We don't have a *domestic little routine*,' she denied, shakily, which made her sound as though she was guiltily denying some earth-shattering, self-evident truth.

'Of course we do! You and Eleanor do homework and chat, and then you both prepare some food and I get home in time to catch up on the last half-hour of family chat...'

'Family chat! Don't be ridiculous!'

Kane raised his eyebrows expressively before pushing himself away. 'We'll leave at three. Will that give you enough time to change before we go to the school?' Having wreaked havoc with her nervous system, he had now resumed his role of thoughtful employer and was looking at her with his head inclined to one side, patiently waiting for her to answer.

Shannon could barely stammer out an affirmative and even the demands of the job, which were usually constant enough to take her mind off everything but literally what was in front of her and needed attention, failed to deliver. Her mind refused to keep to the rails and insisted on breaking its restraints and merrily galloping down Avenue Wild Imagination.

The drive back to the house seemed unnatural at three in the afternoon, when they should both have been at work.

'I feel like a truant,' Kane said, reading her thoughts, and Shannon relaxed enough to smile.

'So do I,' she admitted.

'Do you think we'll get found out and the boss will have us for dinner?'

Shannon laughed at that. Wasn't this what she found most disconcerting? His amazing ability to make her laugh when it was usually his fault that she was in a grumpy mood in the first place? However huge his personal assets were, literally and metaphorically, he still retained a sense of self-irony that could reach out and find the humour behind most things.

'We might,' she said, playing along with the game. 'What do you think we should do if it happens?'

'Throw ourselves at his mercy and beg for forgiveness?'

'Or maybe pretend that our watches were both showing the wrong time and really we thought that it was five-thirty?'

'Ah, we'll be all right.' He gave her a sidelong, teasing look. 'After all, our boss is known to be the fairest, most generous man in London. A paragon amongst the male sex, in fact.'

'Funny. I thought you might reach that conclusion.' She laughed again, and the remainder of the trip back to the house passed by in pleasant silence, broken only by quiet, easygoing conversation that skirted from topic to topic, never resting long enough on any one for it to meander down dangerous byways.

And it was oddly gratifying to dress for a school event. She had been to her brothers' and sisters' various school plays and awards evenings and sports days but she had never attended a school event in the capacity of adult spectator. She wore a green and black checked skirt and a bottle green jumper and her high boots, all fairly new acquisitions since she'd started working for Kane and seen her pay packet considerably increased. She brushed her hair until it shone and then swept it away from her face, pinning it back on either side with two tortoiseshell clips, and was inordinately pleased when Kane told her that she looked absolutely perfect.

And the play was perfect as well. Eleanor remembered all her lines, not that there were that many to remember, and the animals and trees all behaved themselves.

Afterwards, over a fast-food dinner, Shannon recounted her various experiences of school plays and all the disasters that had befallen the various members of her family. When she talked about her past, she could feel it come alive, could feel her excitement as a child as she'd dressed in Nativity costume for a ten-second starring role in the class play. Her eyes sparkled and once or twice, when she looked at Kane, it was to find him staring at her, seemingly enthralled at her recounting of old times. He even joined in with the reminiscences and gave amusing thumbnail sketches of things that had happened to him as a boy.

Eleanor looked gratified but astounded to hear that he'd had a boyhood. Like all children, she probably assumed that her father had mysteriously emerged, fully grown and mature, from his mother's womb.

So it seemed natural, when they had got back to the

house and Eleanor was settled and asleep, to continue the trip down memory lane. And it seemed natural to mention Kane's wife over a cup of frothy coffee. Shannon almost expected him to refuse to answer, but he did, startling her with the length and breadth of his explanation. They met and it had been, he told Shannon, an instant attraction.

'But really,' he said, caressing his coffee-cup thoughtfully, 'when I look back, I wonder whether our mutual infatuation would have matured into something stronger. I don't normally, I assure you, bore people with details of my private life but...' their eyes met and tangled and Shannon's pulse accelerated '...what can I say? We rushed headlong into a relationship and within a year Annette was pregnant. In retrospect, I wonder whether we really ever knew one another that well.'

'What makes you say that?' Shannon asked.

Kane looked at her broodingly. In the muted light, his face was all angles. The shadows lent him a remoteness that was at odds with his frank discussion of his dead wife. 'She was distraught at being pregnant. It wasn't planned and towards the end I could tell that she was terrified that her party days might be over. She was also upset at how her body changed. I always assumed that women found pregnancy enjoyable.' He focused his attention on her, as though indicating that she might be able to provide an answer to this, and Shannon shrugged.

'Not all do. I would, though.' She smiled mistily. 'I can't imagine how wonderful it must be to have a baby growing inside you, feeling it, waiting for it to make its appearance...'

'I thought that might have been your way of looking at things.' There was a lingering silence during which she became aware of the breeze rustling against the window-panes, blowing through the leaves on the trees.

'There's something girlish yet womanly about you.'

'Girlish yet womanly…? What does that mean?' She laughed to dismiss the thick atmosphere between them but found that she couldn't tear her eyes away from his and the laughter died in her throat.

'I guess another way of putting it is…sexy.'

Sexy, sexy.

Sex.

With the man sitting just next to her at the kitchen table.

Shannon licked her lips and Kane watched the unconscious gesture of nervousness, which made her even more nervous. Nervous but excited. Unspeakably excited, in fact.

Then he leant across the few inches separating them and she closed her eyes as his cool lips touched hers.

CHAPTER EIGHT

THIS was what Shannon had been waiting for. The realisation hit her like a bombshell the minute Kane kissed her. It was a slow, lingering kiss. He was tasting her, exploring her mouth with his tongue as his hand reached behind her head, pulling her to him, and Shannon allowed herself to be directed. She was barely aware of the smooth wooden table between them as she leant towards him and into him, drowning in the depths of his mouth. When he finally drew back, she found that she was trembling.

How could he stop? She opened her eyes and saw that he was looking at her.

'What? *What?* What's the matter?' She leaned across and closed her eyes, but he placed one finger very gently on her mouth and her eyes flicked open again.

'We need to talk about this.'

Talk? How could he be contemplating discussion at a time like this?

'Why?' she cried. 'Why do we have to talk about it?'

He sat back in the chair and folded his hands behind his head.

'Look, if you don't want to…if you… I don't turn you on, so what's the point…?' Shannon could feel herself on the brink of tears, but she wouldn't give in. It was obvious. One moment of impulse was now being considered in the harsh glare of reality and found wanting. If he really wanted her, like she really wanted him, he wouldn't have been able to pull back, never mind sit

138

there looking at her through shuttered eyes and telling her that they needed to talk.

She stood up and he said quietly, 'Sit back down, Shannon.'

'And what if I don't?' she flung at him, gripping the edges of the table so fiercely that her knuckles were white. 'What are you going to do? Stop me? So that you can tell me that we need to talk? Drag me back to the kitchen table, kicking and screaming?'

'That,' he said, 'is precisely what I would do.'

By way of reply, she pushed herself back from the table and stalked across the kitchen, her eyes glazed and aching from the effort of not bursting into tears from sheer humiliation. How ironic to think that Eric Gallway, the man she had once idiotically considered the love of her life, had never been able to stir a response like this in her. His seduction had been intense, brief and polished, and his techniques for trying to get her into bed had been much on the same level.

But the stronger he'd tried to fan her flames, the more she'd pulled back, believing that years of indoctrination had given her principles which she couldn't overcome. She had really believed that she couldn't commit to sex before marriage.

If he could see her now! Not a principle in sight. All her principles had vanished over the face of the horizon and she knew, with mounting dismay, that they had vanished because what she felt for Kane Lindley was nothing like what she had felt for Eric Gallway. What she felt was true and strong and right because she was in love with Kane.

The realisation brought a choked lump to her throat. Her eyes were stinging.

She felt his steel-like grip on her wrist before she even realised that he had covered the distance between them.

Shannon stood frozen to the spot, aware of the futility of any physical battle between them. 'Go on, then! Talk! If you want to talk, talk! Get it off your chest.'

'Not here.'

'Why? What difference does it make?'

'In the sitting room.' He didn't give her time to answer. Instead, he pulled her along while she ineffectively tried to wriggle out of his vice-like grip.

The sitting room was in darkness but instead of switching on the overhead lights he flicked on a lamp with one hand while the other remained firmly superglued to her wrist. Then he pulled her along to the sofa and only released her when he was sitting right next to her, close enough for any idea of a quick sprint to the door to be out of the question. Not, she thought, that it mattered. The short distance between the kitchen and the sitting room had been enough for her to consider her options. They were basically limited to two. Attempt a pointless flight from the situation from which she would emerge with her dignity even less intact than it was now, if that was possible, or brazen out her mortifying rejection with as much cold self-possession as she could muster.

'Why don't we just forget what's just happened?' Shannon suggested, staring at the fireplace. She could feel the pulse in her neck beating and she drew in a long, steadying breath. Rallying her defences would be so much easier if she could just ignore the man sitting next to her. He wasn't in her line of vision, but unfortunately she was still intensely aware of his eyes on her. She was also, unfortunately, all too aware of what he was seeing. A woman with heightened colour, her breathing shallow and gasping, hands clammy and shaking. Hardly a vision of cold self-possession, she thought bitterly. More like a vision of total collapse.

'Why would I want to do that?'

'Because we're both adults and adults should be able to deal with mistakes.'

'You're presuming,' Kane said drily, 'that I consider it a mistake.'

'And don't you?' Shannon swung to look at him. Having initially breathed a sigh of relief that the room was in semi-darkness, she now wished that it was bathed in fluorescent light which might have enabled her to read his expression. As it was, his face gave her no clue to his thoughts and she felt like a swimmer, thrashing around in the dark in pursuit of the nearest piece of land. 'Why did you stop, then?'

'Because I need to know that this isn't going to end up being a mistake for you.'

'Very magnanimous of you, Mr Lindley,' Shannon said cuttingly. 'And what about you? What if it turns out to be a mistake for you?'

'I can handle myself.'

'And I can't?'

'Not if your experience with Eric Gallway was anything to go by.'

There he goes again, Shannon thought despairingly. Even on the brink of passion, his wretched sense of consideration took over. Was he like this with all the women he hopped into bed with? Or had he just singled her out as incompetent when it came to taking care of herself? Maybe he was trying to warn her off him. Was that it? Her madly whirring brain tried to deal with every possible hidden meaning behind his attitude and eventually appeared to short circuit.

She gave a short laugh and said sarcastically, 'You certainly know how to kill passion.'

'Oh, is that what I've done?' His dark eyebrows rose beguilingly. 'My passion still seems to be very much alive.'

'Oh, it does, does it?'

'Why don't you find out for yourself if you don't believe me?'

The full extent of her inexperience hit her like a blow and she let out a strangled squeak.

'Sorry, what was that?'

Shannon cleared her throat while her body resisted all attempts at sophistication and went up in flames at the thought of touching him. He was less alarmed at the prospect and he gently took her hand in his and placed it on his lap so that there was now no mistaking the throbbing arousal that told its own story.

'Do I prove my point now?' he asked huskily, and she nodded.

'P-perhaps we should t-talk,' she stuttered, which was rich considering, she thought, that she could barely make her vocal cords get it together to form a sentence, never mind string sentences together to form anything halfway coherent. Every part of her body was actually vibrating, like an engine waiting to race away from the starting post.

'You want to make love with me, don't you, my little flame-haired beauty? I know. I can feel it. I can *smell* it. And I want to make love with you, but if we do, once isn't going to be enough. Not nearly enough.'

His words swam in her head, muffling her thoughts, and she had to fight to concentrate on what he was saying.

'You mean you want to have an affair with me?' she whispered.

'More than that.'

For the merest of split seconds, she was overcome by a swooping sensation of elation as the prospect of marriage flashed on the horizon. Marriage to Kane Lindley, weeks and months and endless years of sharing her love, having his children, basking in the blissful knowledge that they would grow old together, two trees forever entwined.

'I want you to enter into this knowing that we'll be lovers.'

'Lovers? For how long?'

'That's a question without an answer, Shannon.' His voice was gentle. 'I can't and won't make you rash promises of wedding bells and happy-ever-afters and I know you might find that impossible to accept.'

Disappointment was like a wave crashing over her, and it took her less than a second to make her mind up. 'Yes,' she said, closing her eyes. 'Yes, yes, yes.'

'Yes, yes, yes…what? Yes, you find it impossible to accept?'

Shannon opened her eyes to look at him and felt the breath catch in her throat at the thought of all the things they would never share, but they would share enough. He was right, life was hard and there were no happy-ever-afters. All she could hope to do was snatch her piece of happiness while she could and let her dreams take care of themselves.

'Yes. I'll be your lover.' Because I love you, she added silently to herself. Those were dangerous words that would have to be contained, but she could do that because the alternative was turning her back on what her heart needed and yearned for.

Kane smiled and brushed the hair away from her temple. Shannon held his hand, leaning into his palm with her cheek.

'Are you quite sure, my darling?'

'Quite sure.' She leant towards him and opened her mouth against his, taking the initiative to still any further questioning on the subject. This was enough because it would have to be enough, and she could deal with the consequences.

This time there was sweet savagery as his tongue clashed with hers, and when she pressed her hand against him, she could feel him stirring against her, his urgency matching her own. As his mouth left hers, she arched back, groaning as he trailed a path wetly along her neck with his tongue, pausing to tease the tender flesh behind her ears and to tickle her ear with the tip of his tongue.

'What do you like, Shannon?' he asked in a deep, uneven voice. 'What feels good for you?'

'I don't know,' she whispered back. 'But this feels... nice.'

'Just *nice*?' He laughed softly into her ear and his breath sent a shiver through her.

'Well, maybe...wonderful... Would that do?'

'For the moment.' Kane slipped his hand underneath her jumper and delicately traced the outline of her bra, running his fingers along her rib cage, then down to her flat stomach, stopping at the waistband of her skirt. Then he resumed his explorations, down to where her skirt was rucked up against her thigh and then underneath so that the barrier of her flimsy tights felt like iron cladding separating his fingers from her bare flesh.

'But right now,' he murmured, 'I want you to get undressed for me. Very slowly. I want to feast my eyes on every inch of you.'

Shannon stood up and watched him as he watched her. Did he want her to perform a striptease? Instead of feeling nervous at the prospect of that, she felt wantonly erotic. She slowly tugged the jumper over her head and then dropped it to the ground, then undid the zipper of her skirt and stepped out of it, kicking it aside. Then her boots, bending over to release the laces until she could ease them off. No one had ever seen her naked before, not like this.

The excitement was pulsing inside her like waves of hot lava and as she removed her tights she looked up at him and their eyes clashed. Now she was bare other than the lacy flesh-coloured bra and her underwear. She reached behind her, unclasping the bra and letting it fall to join the rest of her clothes. Her instinct was to cover her exposed breasts with her hands, a gesture of modesty, but the naked hunger on his face was an immense turn-on. Instead, she walked towards him and he pulled her to sit on his lap, so that the pointed tips of her nipples were on a level with his mouth.

With a soft sigh, Shannon curled her fingers into his hair and looked down to watch as he suckled at her nipples, drawing first one then the other into his mouth, rubbing his tongue over the sensitive tips until she could barely stand the explosion building up inside her.

'Don't worry, I'm going to take things nice and easy with you...'

As he continued to suck her ripe nipples, hard and engorged now and slick with the wetness of his mouth, his hand moved along her rib cage and he stroked the flat planes of her stomach. Then he slid his hand down beneath the silky elasticised waistband of her underwear, cupping her, and with gentle pressure he rubbed the sensitive mound between her thighs with his palm. Shannon gasped and began to move against his hand, throwing her head back, her mouth half-open as she moaned her pleasure.

'Do you like me touching you there?' he groaned unsteadily into her ear. 'I know you do. You're wet for me.' He eased her off him, laying her flat on the sofa, and she watched as he stood up and began to remove his clothes.

He was as beautiful as she'd imagined he would be. As he stripped off his shirt, she noticed, with feverish excitement, how defined his muscles were. The breadth of his shoulders emphasised the narrowing of his waist and hips and as he stood, finally, in proud nudity for her to absorb, her eyes were drawn to the dark hair curling tenderly at his groin, framing his thrusting erection. She wanted to touch it so badly that she reached out and felt a shudder of heady power as it moved beneath her hand, responding to the lightness of her stroking.

He curled his fingers into her hair and she sat forward to obey his silent command, taking his hardness into her mouth.

'Yes, my darling, just like that.' He controlled the rhythm with his hand on her head. He gave a shudder and tilted her face upwards so that he could look down at her.

'Now, where did you learn to do that?' he asked with a soft, shaky laugh, and Shannon stretched back along the sofa, her arms provocatively raised above her head to hang limply over the edge of the soft cushions.

He pulled her underwear off but, instead of joining her on the massive sofa, he remained standing to stare intimately at her fully unclothed body and Shannon obligingly parted her legs just slightly, enough to afford him the briefest glimpse of her scented womanhood.

They devoured each other with their eyes and when she could bear her mounting need no longer he knelt down and eased her towards him, parting her thighs still wider, then he blew gently between her legs and she whimpered involuntarily.

'You tasted me,' he said, catching her eye and laughing softly as she blushed at the directness of his statement. 'Now it's my turn.'

Kane peeled aside the softly swollen lips sheathing her femininity to expose the small nub, then ran his tongue over it, applying a delicate pressure that made her cry out and buck against his mouth. Her fingers scraped along his shoulders, curled in frenzied passion into his hair, and the delicate pressure became firm strokes.

He eased himself into her so fluidly that Shannon felt not the slightest twinge of discomfort. Her body was ripe and ready for him and his slow thrusts, building up as he moved quicker and faster, brought her to a shuddering climax that seemed to go on for eternity.

Her body was still alive and he gently stroked the flanks of her thighs, as if he were soothing an excited horse. Then, tentatively, he traced the outline of her breast, spiralling his finger in small circles until he was feathering her pink, engorged nipple.

'I think I've developed a taste for you,' he murmured huskily, and she gave a shuddering sigh.

'Is that good or bad?'

'Perhaps I ought to remind myself of it to find out.' He laughed under his breath, a dark, sexy laugh that made her head spin.

Then he pulled her so that she understood what he wanted, easing her along him until his flared nostrils could breath in the musky scent positioned provocatively above his mouth. From her advantageous position, Shannon could see his tongue flick out to touch her sensitised womanhood. Just those delicate flicks were enough to make her arch back and her legs stiffened as his finger moved inside her to touch her deepest depths while his tongue caressed and rubbed until she had to close her eyes, gasping as another orgasm shuddered through her body, as powerful as the first.

This time, as she finally lay beside him, she felt drained. Beautifully drained. There were no thoughts in her head and she might have dozed off if he hadn't spoken, with infinite gentleness.

'I think it's time for bed.'

'Already?' She sighed languorously.

'My bed,' he said gravely, and she gurgled her pleasure.

'But what about Eleanor?'

'Asleep and oblivious. As I'm your boss, it's your duty to comply with my orders.' He cupped her breast in his hand while his thumb stirred her resting nipple into upright alertness.

'Are you saying that I have no choice?' she teased, wriggling on the sofa.

'Correct.'

She giggled and obediently complied. Trusting in the darkness, they grabbed their clothes and hand in hand headed for his bedroom, their footsteps making soft, padding sounds along the carpet.

She had never felt so whole in her life before. The thought that this was simply the start of an affair, no strings attached and no promises given for anything beyond that, was not enough to quell the bubble of joy that had spread through her.

'Are you taking anything…?' he asked, chucking his

clothes on the deep two-seater sofa by the window, and Shannon looked at him blankly.

'Anything like what?'

'Anything like contraception?' he asked.

She hadn't given that a moment's thought. She knew enough about the biological workings of her body, however, to realise that the chances of becoming pregnant were pretty slim. 'I'm in a safe period,' she said quickly. 'Why? Do you think I should go on the Pill? I'm not sure I like the thought of—'

'Shh.' He took her in his arms and cradled her head against his shoulder. 'It's my responsibility as much as yours. If you don't want to take the Pill, I'll make sure I use the necessary protection.'

Shannon closed her eyes and smiled. How could she ever *not* have fallen in love with this man? He made her feel safe, as if his presence could cocoon her against everything unpleasant in the world.

'Don't you mind that I'm so…'

'So what?' He led her towards his king-sized bed and then covered them both with the sprawling duvet, wrapping his big body around her small one so that they were nestled into one another.

'So…hopeless,' Shannon said. 'I mean…well, I bet all the other women you've slept with in the past were on the Pill. I bet you didn't have to worry about accidents happening…'

'You mean apart from my wife…'

'Well, yes.'

He absent-mindedly stroked her thigh and she covered his leg with her own.

'I've always been careful,' he told her thoughtfully. 'It's better to be in control of a situation than to discover down the line that the situation was in control of you…

As to you being hopeless…maybe I like it…' He nuzzled her jawline and then raised himself on his elbows to look down at her. 'You bring out the caveman in me…hadn't you noticed?'

'Mmm. Not sure I like the sound of that…'

'Maybe I mean protector…'

'Oh, yes, I can see that,' Shannon said wryly. 'My mother's surprise visit was proof enough.'

'And how pleased she would be to know that I'm going to carry on protecting you,' he told her smugly. 'Keep my eye on you, stop you from straying off the straight and narrow…'

'Thrilled, I'm sure,' she said with a laugh.

But, she thought to herself, that was a little piece of information she definitely would be keeping to herself.

More difficult, she thought three weeks later as she walked into her office, was keeping it from all her friends at work. No one had said anything, but Shannon was sure that they'd noticed the difference between herself and Kane. For a start, he came to the office canteen for lunch whenever he happened to be in the building, and instead of discreetly sitting at a distant table, out of sight, he always made sure to sit where she was, seemingly oblivious to any abrupt silences that greeted his arrival. Lunching with the head honcho reduced even the most garrulous to awed, stuttering silence.

'People will suspect,' Shannon had told him the week before.

'Suspect what?' He had moved across to perch on her desk and idly played with a strand of her hair.

'Suspect what's going on.'

'Why?'

'Because you never used to go to the canteen before?

Because you always come and sit where I am? Because most people can add two and two and get four?'

'I'm just a good boss,' he'd said soothingly, 'taking an interest in what's going on on the ground floor.' And that had been the end of that.

'Christmas,' he said, as soon as she walked into his office with his ritual cup of coffee, very strong and black.

Shannon was now well accustomed to his lack of preliminaries when it came to conversation.

'Two weeks' time.' She sat primly in the chair, facing him, and felt that familiar stirring as he leaned back in the swivel chair and looked at her from under his lashes.

'I want you to stay here with me. With us.'

'I can't,' she said with a little sigh. 'Mum would hit the roof.'

'We could go away. Somewhere hot. Two weeks in the Maldives. Wouldn't it be nice? Making love on a beach every night?'

'Every night?' She blushed and he pushed himself away from the desk and patted his lap invitingly.

'I bet you've never done it on a bed of sand before...'

'You know I haven't.'

'Come and sit closer and tell me why you won't consider it.'

'We can't...not here, Kane...not in the office... What if...?'

That was another thing she had become accustomed to. The deceptively chivalrous nature that fooled you into thinking that all his actions were ruled by an inner code of good behaviour. In public perhaps, but in bed, he threw off that mantle and was thrillingly primitive in his love-making. He was also thrillingly inventive.

'You worry too much, my sweet,' he said, crooking

his finger for her to come to him. 'The outer door is closed, isn't it?'

'Well, yes, but…' She glanced nervously over her shoulder and obediently sidled around the desk to be yanked down forcefully on his lap.

'But nothing, woman. Can't you see how much you turn me on? I can't see you without wanting you. I amaze myself by even being able to work fairly normally when I know you're only a matter of a few feet away.' He unbuttoned her decorous blouse and groaned when he saw that she wasn't wearing a bra. 'Was this for me?' he asked, cupping her breasts in both his hands, weighing them and then opting to lick and suck her left nipple while she cradled his dark head in her hands.

'My bras don't seem to fit any more,' Shannon said in little pants.

'Good. Get rid of the lot. Mmm. And your nipples look bigger as well. Maybe they're responding to frequent use…' He demonstrated his definition of 'use' by virtually making love to her breasts until she was squirming on his lap. 'For a lady who was so concerned about being caught in a compromising position,' he told her huskily, 'you've managed to shed your inhibitions pretty quickly. Not, my little wanton hussy, that you have any inhibitions…'

He paused to reach into his drawer and Shannon scolded him reprovingly but indulgently as he withdrew a condom, shifting her so that he could unzip his trousers and slip it over his hardness, already fully erect and hungry for satisfaction. He had been true to his word. After the first time, he'd taken no chances of any unwanted pregnancy; no sex without protective measures.

But before Kane could slide into her, he raised her skirt, pulled her underwear to one side and inserted his

tongue into the apex between her thighs, doing there
what he did so well, driving her insane with desire as
his tongue flicked and explored and delicately probed
the pulsating, acutely sensitive nub. It was agony having
to be pleasured without moaning out loud but heaven
only knew what the fall-out would have been if someone
had happened to innocently open the outer door to the
sounds of elevated groaning coming from the direction
of Kane's office!

Then he sat her on him and gripped her firm buttocks
as they lost themselves in the furious business of wild
gratification.

'Will that be all, Mr Lindley?' Shannon whispered
into his ear, head on his shoulder, eyes half closed with
pure happiness.

'Why, I do believe my perfect little secretary is going
to corrupt me with all of this. Quite unorthodox, my
dear.'

'You only have yourself to blame. I learnt from the
hands of a master.' She blew into his hair and he clasped
his arm more tightly around her waist.

'If you insist on abandoning me for Christmas,' he
said softly, with little-boy petulance that made her want
to laugh, 'then at least go for the shortest time possible.'

'I *am* allowed a fortnight's leave from work, sir, according to company policy...'

'Are you now?' He looked at her as if disbelieving
the source of her information. 'Actually, I only work it
out as a week...'

'Uh. I'll think about it.' Shannon reluctantly straightened herself, at the end of which she still felt wickedly
debauched.

'And I expect phone calls every day.'

'Or else what? Sir?' She resumed her correct position

at the chair in front of his desk and inclined her head curiously to one side.

'Or else you may find an unexpected and sex-starved visitor at your mother's door...' At which he saw fit to conclude the conversation with a glimmer of a smile on his lips and begin proceedings for the day.

It was only three days later, after a Christmas tree had been mounted amid much excitement from Eleanor, that something occurred to Shannon.

She hadn't had her period recently. Her timekeeping when it came to her periods tended to be lax but she was sure that something should have happened already.

By the following morning, as she slunk into the nearest chemist's during her lunch hour, she was in a state of thinly suppressed panic. Once. They had made love once without protection, and by her calculations it hadn't been during a fertile period. She didn't think. She hoped.

She bought the pregnancy kit and secreted it in her office, relieved that Kane was tied up in meetings and nowhere to be seen. She waited in gut-wrenching anxiety until five o'clock rolled around and she could straighten her desk and head back to the house.

Actually taking the thing out of the bag and using it brought Shannon slap bang into the darker side of reality which she had blissfully spent the past few weeks ignoring. The fact that, however much she loved Kane Lindley, the love was one way only. Even at the heights of passion, when men, she had once read, were wont to make declarations of a love they didn't feel, he had remained silent on the subject. He wanted her, he lusted after her, he enjoyed her company and he had no hesitation in telling her as much. But love?

In the silence of her bathroom, while Eleanor was downstairs doing her homework, she sat and watched while fate came home to stay. She was pregnant. The clear blue line in the pregnancy box was unequivocal.

Shannon hadn't expected it. She'd bought the kit, she'd played with the vague notion but, looking at that determined blue line, she realised now that she hadn't expected to be pregnant at all.

The unexpected accident had happened and all the time they had been blithely making love, using protection, she'd been pregnant. She felt as though somewhere up in the heavens, the gods were watching her and snorting with laughter.

She felt a wave of nausea replace shock. What would Kane say to this sudden development in what was supposed to be a light-hearted affair with no strings attached? Pregnancy wasn't merely a string. It was a thick rope and she tried and failed to picture his reaction. He would want to take responsibility. That was the type of man he was. He might even ask her to marry him. The prospect of a marriage made under these circumstances was enough to make her blood run cold. She couldn't think straight while she was under his roof. She needed time to work out some kind of plan before she broke the news to him.

It wasn't yet six o'clock and she knew that he wouldn't be back for at least another hour, probably a bit more.

Shannon picked up the telephone and after a shaky phone call to Carrie, who wasn't best pleased at the favour being asked of her, she went downstairs and explained to Eleanor that she had to leave on important family business. When she said that she would be back as soon as she could, she made sure to superstitiously cross her fingers behind her back. Carrie, she said, was on her way over.

Eleanor listened and then said, 'Are you feeling all right? You don't look very well. You're not ill, are you?'

The smile Shannon offered Eleanor in response to this question was glassy and unfocused.

'No! No, of course not! It's just...' she mumbled. 'Mum, actually. Bit of an accident around the house. Vacuuming. Broken ankle. Fell over the, um, vacuum.'

Eleanor looked perplexed at this explanation but let it go. 'What shall I tell Dad?'

'I'll call him. You just tell him that I'll be in touch.'

CHAPTER NINE

SHANNON lay on her bed and stared up at the ceiling. It was something she had been doing quite a bit of over the past three days. Her mother had given up asking her what was wrong since the standard answer Shannon supplied was, 'nothing, Mum.' She had also, thankfully, stopped asking how 'that nice young man of yours' was. If she was disturbed at her daughter's vague responses as to how long she intended to stay in Ireland, she kept her unease to herself.

But Shannon knew that her mother was worrying. And she thought that she would have plenty more to worry about if she only knew the full extent of the situation. One pregnant daughter, one 'nice young man' who would promptly turn into a monster the minute she knew that he was the father and one job in London which would be no more.

She sighed heavily and felt her eyes begin to well up again. Crying was also high on her list of sudden idiosyncrasies. If it weren't for the fact that she had to maintain a cheerful façade whenever she was with her family, she seriously reckoned that she would be crying all the time. Her bedroom would become a swimming pool. And she still hadn't managed to work out what she was going to do.

Returning to London wasn't an option. Naturally, she would have to tell Kane about her condition, but when she thought too hard about that she could feel herself braking violently at the prospect and cravenly telling herself that there was no need for immediate revelations. She would get a job first, find somewhere to live because living under her mother's roof would be impossible and then present him with a *fait accompli*. Except, what job? She couldn't think offhand of any employers who would hire a pregnant woman with open arms. Not unless they were mad. Which would mean temp work. Which would mean no money. Which would mean no independence. The sigh became a groan of despair.

From downstairs she became aware of her mother calling her and Shannon heaved herself up from the comfort of her bed and reluctantly went to her door and shouted.

'I'll be down in a minute, Mum! I'm just...' What was she just doing? Meditating? 'Cleaning up my bed-room!' She looked around her and decided that she would really get her act together very soon and actually do something about the state of it. Her bed was unmade and her brother, who had been ousted amid much pro-test, had not seen fit to tidy up his clothes and neither had she.

'Well, come down now!'

The voice had come nearer. In a minute, knowing her mother, she would come and fetch her down. Shannon grudgingly went downstairs and trailed limply in the di-rection of the kitchen, bypassing the small lounge which the family used as a television room and from which came boisterous noises of her brothers who seemed to spend most of their free time playing weird games on the television with their friends.

'You have a visitor.' Her mother appeared in front of her with a rolling-pin in one hand and a bowl in the other.

'Who?' At six-thirty in the evening, she couldn't think

of anyone who might be visiting her. No one knew she was around, apart from her family.

'You haven't been sleeping again, have you?' her mother asked suspiciously, and Shannon went pink.

'Why would I be sleeping at this ridiculous hour, Mum? I told you, I was cleaning the bedroom. It's a tip. You have to tell Brian to move his clothes out. I can't find anything.'

'There seems no point to that, Shannon, when you haven't deigned to tell us how long you're going to be here.' She looked as though she might say more, but she had already said it. On a number of occasions. Usually with a level of concern in her voice that brought on an instant attack of crippling guilt.

'Well, who's my surprise visitor? Can't you tell them that I'm not well?' She hung back from the kitchen door, alarmed at the prospect of having to be sociable when all she wanted to do was curl up like a ball and hide.

'No, I can't. You do your own dirty work, Shannon.' With which she strode away, with her daughter following miserably in her wake. 'And let me tell you right off that I'm sick to death of you moping around this house as though the sky's fallen in. You put a smile on your face, my girl!'

Shannon grimaced.

'That's better. Not much, but better.'

Shannon was still sporting the sinister grimace on her face when she pushed open the kitchen and froze in her tracks. Her legs refused to propel her any further and her heart seemed to do something funny.

'Your visitor,' her mother introduced triumphantly, doubtless, Shannon thought numbly, expecting her to be pleased, thrilled, over the moon. After all, hadn't the 'nice young man' whose name Shannon had refused to mention, followed her all the way from London to Ireland?

Kane was sitting at one end of the long, weathered kitchen table with a cup of tea in his hand, while her mother rolled pastry at the other end. A cosy scene. He looked perfectly at ease in a pair of black jeans and a thick, black jumper, the sleeves of which he had pushed up to the elbows to accommodate the warmth in the kitchen. Shannon felt her heart begin to do a panicky quickstep.

'Well, aren't you going to say hello?' Her mother paused in her pastry-rolling to shoot Shannon a lethal look that spoke volumes.

'Uh, hello,' Shannon said, hovering uncertainly by the door. Her hands began to stray guiltily to her stomach and she clasped them firmly behind her back. 'How are you?'

'Fine.' He spoke at last. It was bad enough seeing him but she dreaded hearing that deep voice.

'Cup of tea, love?' her mother asked, and Shannon shuffled into the kitchen, managing to somehow walk sideways, like a crab, towards the kettle.

'So, what are you doing here?'

'I came to see how your mother was.'

'How *I* was?'

'Apparently,' Kane drawled, not taking his cool eyes off Shannon's flushed face, 'you broke your ankle, tripping over the vacuum.'

The lie rebounded off the walls of the kitchen and then subsided into deafening silence.

'Ah.' Shannon cleared her throat. 'As you can see, Mum's fine.'

'What's going on here?' Rose asked. She stopped rolling altogether and proceeded to dish out one of her spectacularly penetrating glares at Shannon. 'What's all this nonsense about broken ankles and vacuum cleaners?'

'Oh, dear,' Kane said in a voice dripping with false innocence, 'have I put my foot in it?'

'Shannon, you look at me. Have you been telling untruths?'

'Sort of.' At which point the kettle began whistling furiously and she busied herself with making a cup of tea, taking her time, while two pairs of eyes were focused on her conscience-stricken back.

'You seem to have a nasty habit of sort of telling untruths, don't you, reds?'

Shannon swung to look at him and found him standing right there beside her like a dark, avenging angel, which was crazy because he didn't know anything. *Go and sit back down,* she wanted to yell. *Go where I don't have to breathe you in.*

'You shouldn't have come here,' she whispered shakily.

'Why should I leave you to crawl away? I've done you a favour, reds. There's guilt stamped all over your face. If I hadn't shown up, you would have been living with your guilt for ever.'

'I have nothing to be guilty about!'

'And is that another sort of untruth?' He removed the bottle of milk from her shaking hands and poured some into her cup.

She was temporarily saved from the necessity of having to enlarge on that explanation by the thundering sound of boisterous young boys who pelted into the kitchen and stopped in their tracks.

'Oh, hi,' Brian said, looking at Kane with devouring curiosity. 'Mum, when's tea? We're hungry.' His three friends shuffled about in the kitchen, peering around for anything edible on offer. 'And the computer's crashed.'

'Who's the visitor?' Brian asked.

'Kane Lindley.' Kane was looking at the assorted, badly dressed heap of fourteen-year-old boys with amusement. 'Your sister's employer.'

'When is she going back to London? She's in my room.'

'No, Brian, I'm actually in *my* room.'

'It's not your room any longer.'

His friends began hooting and jeering and making disgusting noises, and heaven only knew how long their juvenile antics would have carried on if Kane hadn't stood up and informed them that he would have a look at the computer.

All four pelted out of the kitchen in a reverse stampede, followed by Kane who paused only to say to Shannon, 'I'll leave you to chat with your mother, shall I? You probably have one or two things to say by way of explanation.'

'So,' her mother said, once the kitchen door was shut. 'What's Kane doing here?'

'He said you vanished without notice and he came to find out if anything was wrong.'

'You see what I mean!' Shannon cried out, clutching her mug. 'Didn't I tell you that this would happen the minute I made the mistake of taking him up on his offer to live under his roof while I looked for somewhere else? Didn't I tell you?'

She thought of Eleanor, who had enjoyed every minute of her company, and the pleasure she had shared with Kane before circumstances had taken a turn for the worse, and felt herself flush with guilt. It was easier to deal with him, though, if she could work herself up to a fury so she doggedly fanned the little spark of self-righteous anger until she was feeling suitably hard done by.

'I don't need anyone chasing me up here to find out what's going on when nothing's going on! I was due to have some holiday leave anyway! I didn't choose to move to London so that I could end up in a situation with someone checking on my every movement!'

'He said you disappeared without any explanation. Apart from this nonsense, presumably, about my broken ankle, tripping over a household gadget. Did something happen there that I should know about? Sit down, Shannon and stop hovering there by the counter. Sit down and talk to me.'

She finished putting the pastry over the chicken pie which she popped into the oven, then she wiped her floury hands on her apron and sat down.

'The last time I spoke to you on the phone, you sounded very happy. So what happened to you in the space of one week?'

'Nothing. I just…needed a bit of space…'

'So you flew back here, where there's no peace and quiet to be found with those mad brothers of yours stamping through the house like elephants. Spin me another fairy-tale, Shannon.'

'I felt homesick,' Shannon said.

Now was the perfect time to tell her mother everything. She would be shocked and disappointed at first, but she would also be supportive. There was nothing to fear in that respect. But she just couldn't. The conditions, she decided, were not optimum. She needed to have her mother to herself for her confession. It couldn't be done when Kane was outside and four adolescents were waiting to burst into the kitchen again in another feeding frenzy. She would take her mother out for tea, perhaps tomorrow, when Kane had gone, and she would tell her everything then.

'It gets lonely down in London,' she elaborated, playing loosely with the truth, 'especially at Christmas. I mean, Mum, Christmas is special here at home. All of us together. I just gave in to a fit of nostalgia. You could say.'

'Why didn't you tell Kane that? Instead of having the poor man rush up here, thinking you'd been taken ill?'

'He thought I'd been taken ill?' Shannon asked anxiously. 'Did he tell you that? That I was sick?'

He couldn't suspect anything, could he? No, she thought, men's minds didn't operate like that. And there had been no signs. No sudden bursts of unexplained nausea, no strange food cravings, nothing suspicious. Just as well she'd found out early, before she'd begun to put on weight. Just as well she hadn't gone on the Pill after all after that first time. Shannon considered the consequences of that and shuddered. She'd accepted the fact of the baby inside her from the very first moment of discovery, and what she felt wasn't a sense of despondency or of hopes shattered but, strangely, one of rapture that she would now have something to show for her love, a child she could treasure, a lasting memory of the only man she would ever love.

'Not in so many words, but he was obviously concerned.'

'I did contact him after I left,' Shannon said truthfully. Actually, she'd left a message on his answering machine at home when she'd known he would be at work, telling him that she was very busy but would be in touch as soon as Christmas was out of the way. 'Did he say when he would be leaving?'

'He didn't. And I didn't see fit to ask him. I wouldn't want him thinking that he was unwelcome here after all that he did for you.'

'Well, it won't be overnight. He has to get back to Eleanor.'

'Why don't *you* ask him, then?'

'Ask me what?'

Typically, Kane had given no advance warning of his reappearance in the kitchen. He hadn't even knocked! So much for exquisite, gentlemanly good manners. Shannon looked at her mother to see whether she had noticed that oversight, but her mother was smiling. Lord, did this man know how to worm his way under people's skin!

'Shannon was just wondering how long you were going to be here,' her mother said guilelessly, 'because she wanted to take you to a new Italian restaurant that's opened just outside Dublin. Very near here, in fact. Give you two a chance to talk. There'll be no opportunity here, that's for sure.'

'Oh, was she now?' Kane murmured. He shot her a telling look and smiled. 'Well, you're in luck, Shannon, as it happens. I booked to stay overnight in a hotel and it would be my pleasure to be taken out for a meal.'

'Well…I…' Shannon stalled.

'I know,' her mother said, reaching over to pat her hand, 'you're worried about lack of transport. Well, love, you're welcome to my car. It's only an old thing,' she explained to Kane, 'but it goes and it's very reliable. And taxis can be very unreliable at this time of year unless you book one in advance. Of course, you'll have to change, Shannon. You look a state in those clothes. Whatever possessed you to walk around the house in those faded jeans and great, baggy jumper?' She clucked her tongue reprovingly.

'Shall I make a reservation? For, let's say, eight?'

'I'll just fetch the number for you.' Her mother inspected various assorted cards attached by magnets to the fridge door and pulled one off. 'Very handy that I kept this, wouldn't you agree, Shannon? Hilary went there only last week and was so impressed that she gave me the card. Not that an old woman like me gets to go out to fancy places.'

Shannon felt like a cornered rabbit.

'In which case, I'm sure Kane wouldn't mind if you came with us!' she said, inspired.

'I wouldn't dream of it.' Her mother firmly squashed any such hopeful suggestion. 'I wouldn't leave these young lads in this house unsupervised if my life depended on it. Don't know what the state of the place would be when I got back! No, love, you two go and have a good time. Now, you get upstairs and do something with yourself, there's a good girl.'

So, left without a choice, Shannon stamped upstairs, pausing *en route* to look in on Brian who gave her a thumbs-up because evidently the computer had been fixed.

'He's pretty cool,' Ronan said, winking conspirationally at her. 'Better than the last cretin you went out with.'

'Thank you, Ronan,' Shannon scowled, 'but when I want the opinions of a minor, I'll ask.'

Which resulted in the predictable roaring of four adolescents with nothing, she thought, better to do than make loud, suggestive noises at the slightest opportunity.

When she reappeared half an hour later it was to find

Kane and her mother ensconced in the sitting room, poring over photo albums.

'My fault,' Kane said, standing up and countering her sour glance with an unrepentant grin. 'I begged your mother to take a trip down memory lane.'

'Not that I needed much persuasion!'

'What a wonderful way to pass the time,' Shannon said with a little scowl. She was wearing an old, long-sleeved, black woollen dress, one of the few items in her wardrobe not in need of ironing thanks to Brian's cavalier treatment of all her clothes which had been bundled up into a trunk in the corner of the bedroom.

'And informative,' Kane added, walking towards her and helping her on with her coat.

She muttered cattily under her breath, 'Especially to nosy people like you.'

'Now, now,' he whispered silkily into her ear, 'you won't get rid of me by being nasty. I'm a persistent guy. I thought you would have known that by now.'

In retrospect, she thought as they drove through icy weather to the restaurant, his persistence was the one factor she hadn't reckoned on. She thought that he would have waited for her to contact him, but she should have known that Kane Lindley didn't wait for people to do things. If it suited him, he would simply intervene and would then proceed to bludgeon through all obstacles until he got what he wanted.

The drive was completed in silence. She'd demanded silence because she'd said that she would need all her concentration to get them to the restaurant in an unfamiliar car in wintry driving conditions. Obligingly, he said not one word, even though her fertile imagination conducted a conversation of its own, formulating imaginary questions from him and then sifting through the various answers she could give him.

The restaurant, when they arrived twenty minutes later, was pleasantly crowded. With snow predicted, the weather had kept some people away so that it wasn't packed to the rafters, and they were shown to a table at the back. It didn't have the elegance of some of the London restaurants, but there was a pleasing informality about it. In fact, it reminded her of Alfredo's.

'So, reds,' Kane said, after he'd ordered some wine and mineral water, 'have you missed me? You look a bit peaky. Have you been pining?'

She hadn't expected that question for an opening gambit. In fact, she thought that he might have gone immediately into accusatory mode, with her mother no longer around to put a brake on his self-control, and had consequently prepared a mental list of all possible answers to deal with accusations.

'I don't feel peaky,' she hedged, pretending to give the menu her full attention.

'That's not what I asked.'

'Don't tell me that you flew to Ireland to find out whether I was missing you or not.'

'Why? Is it that inconceivable?'

'Yes, as a matter of fact.' She snapped shut the menu and linked her fingers together on her lap. 'I'm going to have the soup, followed by the cannelloni. What about you?'

He ignored her weak attempt to steer the conversation out of choppy waters. 'Why? Don't you think that your sudden absence might have left a dent in my life?'

'I think it may have left a dent in your ego,' Shannon told him. 'Look, perhaps I shouldn't have run out like that. I know it was rude but, um, I suddenly got cold feet. Anyway, I did leave a message for you on your answering machine. Didn't you get it?'

'Oh, I got it all right. I just wasn't too impressed with it.'

'Why not? I told you I'd be in touch.' When he didn't say anything, she rushed on, 'Maybe I should have spoken to you in person, but I didn't think at the time. I just felt as though I had to get away...'

'In which case, why did you lie and tell Eleanor that your mother had tripped and broken her ankle?'

'Well, I wasn't about to tell her that her father and I had been lovers, was I?' The words sent a warm flush spreading across her cheeks and she gratefully watched the progress of the waiter towards them. Any distraction to relieve her of her cross-examination.

They ordered their food and Kane waited in polite silence until wine had been poured and glasses filled with mineral water.

'You're blushing,' he commented mildly. 'Does it still make you go hot under the collar when you think about us making love? Does your skin still tingle when you think about me touching you?'

'Why are you asking me these questions?' She felt herself go a deeper, brighter shade of red. 'Why don't you just get to the point? I know you're angry with me.'

'Do I look as if I'm angry with you?'

Shannon sneaked a look at his face. No, he didn't look angry, but he must be. In fact, she desperately hoped that he was because it would make her life a whole lot easier.

'How do you think I felt when I got back home to find that you'd disappeared? Eleanor was upset. She didn't understand and she didn't believe you when you told her that lie about having to rush back to Ireland to see about your mother's ankle. She may only be eight, but children are very clever when it comes to reading between the lines.'

'Yes, I know, and I'm sorry about that.' Shannon's guilt was fast reaching overwhelming proportions. 'I just couldn't think of anything else to say.' She thought of Eleanor's trusting face and felt a pang of excruciating misery. 'I wasn't thinking straight at the time.'

'Why not?' he moved in swiftly, his eyes narrowing. 'That's what I don't understand. Why you suddenly felt the need to run away. If you wanted to tell me that you weren't happy with…us, why couldn't you have waited until the morning instead of rushing out of the house in a panic?'

'Because…because…' Shannon thought wildly, wondering what she could come up with that would turn desperate, irrational behaviour into something reasonable.

'Take your time. I'm in no hurry.'

'Why can't you understand that some people act on impulse?' she cried desperately. She daren't meet his eyes. She hardly dared look at him, in fact, because there was no part of him that didn't fill her with memories. 'Not everyone thinks things through and then behaves in a rational manner! Some of us just do things on the spur of the moment! It's just another reason why you and I are so ill suited, why we have nothing in common. *Nothing!*'

'I can think of quite a few things we have in common.'

'And I'm not talking about sex!' Shannon attacked swiftly.

'Nor am I!' He leant forward and forced her to look at him, forced her to meet his glittering black eyes. 'I can't imagine how little Eleanor and I meant for you to just disappear like a bloody thief in the night, woman!'

'What's the point trying to defend myself when you won't even try to understand?'

'I understand that you're a coward...'

As she was feverishly trying to come up with an answer to that, the waiter produced their starters and she fell on hers with the enthusiasm of someone saved by the bell.

'So, reds, want to pretend that everything's all right? Fine. Let's behave like civilised adults and pretend, shall we? Make polite conversation for a while?' He gave a mirthless laugh. 'How does it feel, being back in Ireland?' He sighed, as though he couldn't help himself, and ran his hands wearily over his eyes.

Shannon didn't care whether he was humouring her. She grabbed the lifeline with alacrity.

'Weird.' Her voice was high and unreal. He looked shaken. Was he hurting? She wanted to reach out and stroke his hand, make believe that everything was going to be all right. Instead, she took a few deep breaths and concentrated on her garlic prawns. 'Also, Brian had taken over my bedroom and he was put out when I turned up because now he's sharing with Ronan again.'

'Sometimes it's hard to return to the family nest when you've flown it, isn't it, reds?' he murmured roughly.

Shannon relaxed and told herself that perhaps the worst of their confrontation was now over. When she tried to think ahead, she wondered how he would react when he learnt of the pregnancy. If he could follow her to Ireland simply because he wanted one or two questions answered, what would he do when he discovered that he was going to be a father? She would have to delay the revelation, she thought. For his sake.

'And what have you been doing since you got back? Going out much?' There was a curiously flat inflection to his voice, but his expression remained watchful.

'Now and again,' Shannon said vaguely. 'I've felt a bit…tired recently, so I've been staying put quite a bit.'

'Tired?'

'Just lethargic,' Shannon said hurriedly, intercepting any possible questions about her health. 'Must be the weather. Winter is awful for making me want to hibernate. Is Carrie with Eleanor?'

Kane nodded and sat back to allow his main course to be placed in front of him. Roast cod, surrounded by vegetables. He almost always ate fish when out. It was an unimportant titbit of information that made her feel suddenly nostalgic. How much else had she stored away in her memory about him that would jump out and surprise her over the years to come?

'So you'll be heading back…in the morning?'

'Around lunchtime, actually.'

'Oh.'

'And what about you?'

'Me? What about me?'

'When do you intend to head back to London? Or do you intend to head back at all?'

Shannon tried to feel infuriated that he was pinning her down when she should have the freedom to make her own choices, but she couldn't. She just thought about him leaving and her having to cope on her own without his sense of humour and intelligence and conversation to carry her along.

'I don't know if…' she said weakly.

'I hope you wouldn't let me put you off coming back, because it was well within your right to kill our affair.'

'I didn't want to kill anything,' Shannon blurted out,

reddening as he digested her outburst without saying anything.

'No,' he agreed softly, 'you didn't, did you?'

Shannon shook her head and gave a long, resigned sigh. Well, it had worked. She had fallen straight into his ambush and it had worked a treat. He had been so nice, so understanding to have stopped quizzing her about her abrupt departure that she had dropped her guard, and it was only been a matter of time before he got the truth out of her. She knew him but, conversely, he knew her, too. He knew her well enough to realise that arguing would have put her back up so he hadn't argued. She was overcome by a feeling that none of it mattered any more anyway.

'So tell me why you concocted that story about getting cold feet. You don't have to have any secrets from me. You can share what's really on your mind. I'm not going to punish you so there's no need to feel as though you have to run away. Problems don't evaporate because you choose to run away from them. In fact, it's been my experience that the faster you run from a problem the larger it looms on the horizon.'

'I *did* get cold feet, Kane.' She knew that every word he was saying was true, he didn't know how true, but she just couldn't face him with the full truth. 'I didn't *want* to end it, but I...' She placed her knife and fork very precisely together and then rested her elbows on the table and stared down disconsolately at the uneaten food on her plate.

'I realised that I'm not cut out for an affair after all. I thought that I would be able to handle it, but I can't. When I went down to London, I was determined to grow up, I guess. I mean, I'm hardly a teenager any more, am I? That's what happens, I think, when you grow up in a family as large as mine. You're so cushioned against everything that you just don't have to mature as quickly as other people the same age as you.'

'Or maybe it's just easier to go with the flow. You don't have to make decisions if there are other people around who will make them for you. London must have been a shock for you, Shannon.'

She shrugged. 'At any rate, I thought I could behave like the sophisticated woman I never will be so, yes, I ran away.'

'So if you don't want an affair, what *do* you want?'

'Some coffee?' She laughed nervously.

He allowed the flippancy to pass and ordered two cups of cappuccino which arrived with a little plate of interestingly shaped chocolates and biscuits.

'You haven't answered my question.'

'Yes, I have!' Shannon squirmed in the chair and then spooned some of the milky froth into her mouth. 'I told you why I ran away like I did. I wanted to be one kind of person but I'm not.'

'But I know all that,' Kane said gently. His gentleness was unnerving. He should be hurling criticism at her, not sitting there making her believe that he understood.

'What do you mean, you know all that? You don't know me at all!'

'Oh, yes, I do. I know you better than you know yourself.'

'Trust you to say something like that.'

'You mean I'm predictable?' He laughed softly. 'We'll have to do something about that, then, won't we?'

Shannon's heart gave an unhealthy flutter of excitement. He reached out and lightly covered her hand with his, stroking it with his thumb.

'We will?' she found herself weakly compelled to ask.

'Oh, yes. Why do you think I travelled all this way?' He sipped his coffee and looked at her narrowly over the rim of the cup. When Shannon took her own cup in her hands, she could feel her fingers trembling.

'Because you were annoyed that I left without any explanation?'

'We're back to this dented ego thing, aren't we? I didn't come here because I was mad with rage and suffering from wounded pride because you walked out on me. I came here to take you back where you belong.'

'You haven't heard a word I've just said!'

'I've heard every word, reds. Of course, I'm still waiting for the three you haven't said. Those three little words that made you run away like you did.'

'I...' Shannon looked at him sulkily. 'I...I love you, Kane Lindley.'

'Now, that wasn't so hard, was it?'

'I'm still not coming back to London to be your mistress,' Shannon said hotly.

'And I wouldn't ask you to. I've come to take you back with me so that you can be my wife.'

CHAPTER TEN

'YOUR wife?' Shannon looked at Kane incredulously.

'That's right.' He signalled for the bill and then smiled at her, a smile that sent her fluttering heart soaring upwards, somewhere in the region of the heavens.

'Shouldn't that proposal be accompanied by three little words?'

'Rather more than three.' He stopped talking to sign the credit card slip, then leant across the table towards her. 'But I'll just start by saying that I love you.'

'But you can't. Can you? Really? Are you...sure?' She looked at him anxiously. If there was a fly in the ointment, then it was important that she find out sooner rather than later. 'But you said that an affair with me was no promise of a wedding ring, you told me that it was a relationship without commitment.'

'And I believed it at the time, I assure you.' He shook his head, as if marvelling at the way events had altered the course he had originally planned. 'But,' he told her as they walked out to the car, 'I was wrong. By nature, I have always been a considered man. You know that, don't you? I've been accustomed to using my head rather than my heart, especially after my last marriage when I realised, somewhat late in the day, that impulse has a nasty habit of backfiring when you least expect it.' He switched on the engine but, instead of pulling away, he turned to her, resting his arm along the back of her seat. It had begun to snow, light flurries like powder than brushed against the windscreen. Stray people on the

176

streets hurtled along, heads bent, hands clutching tightly
at their coats in an attempt to protect themselves from
the freezing weather. Inside the car, with the engine on,
it was warm.

'I thought I could handle anything. I thought that marriage was a step I wouldn't take until I was one hundred
per cent sure it would be the right step. I failed to realise,
until you ran out on me, that I had been one hundred
per cent sure for longer than I cared to think. Do you
know that you were the reason I kept coming back to
Alfredo's every morning?'

'Me?'

He laughed softly at the incredulity in her voice. 'You.
I was on my way to a breakfast meeting at a client and
I stopped in for a quick coffee and a chance to look over
some files. And there you were, with your red hair and
your Irish voice and that way you had of looking as
though any requests for a refill of coffee might result in
a heated debate. In the end, I didn't get through nearly
as much work as I'd anticipated, and I found myself
going back the next morning and every morning after
that, even though the damn place was hardly convenient.
I began to look forward to seeing you in the mornings,
before my day had begun, bursting with vitality, always
ready to make comments on my choice of newspaper or
some item of news that might have captured your interest. There were times I caught myself wondering what
you did for the rest of the day, where you went, who
you saw, what the quality of your personal life was
like...'

'You never said...'

'On a conscious level, I don't think I was aware of it
myself at the time. But I do know that when you threw
that plate of food over Gallway, I felt myself want to

laugh in a way I couldn't remember wanting to laugh in a very long time.'

'But you didn't.'

'No, I didn't. I offered you a job instead.' He brushed her hair back with his fingers and then gently pulled her towards him. When his mouth found hers, she was powerfully aware that this was where she belonged. Wrapped up and possessed by this big, strong man who could admit to feelings most men might want to hide, to being vulnerable in a way that assumed unswerving trust in her response.

'And it was the best damn thing I ever did,' he murmured into her mouth, before resuming his kiss. 'I should have thanked that arrogant little twerp for handing me the opportunity to have you near me. Although if I'd known your connection with him at the time, I might have been tempted to kill him on the spot.'

He slipped his hand under the lapels of her thick coat and moaned huskily as he found the mound of her breast, primly concealed by the woollen dress but, even so, responding to the hot touch of his hand.

'Is there a law in Ireland against making passionate love in the back seat of a car?' he demanded, nibbling her ear lobe. 'Because if there is, I have a rather nice hotel room booked and we have some catching up to do…'

'Kane…'

The fly in the ointment, which had been dormant during his heady, blissful protestations of love, now began to buzz. Gently at first, but then with increasing vigour. A nasty, frightening thought lodged in her mind. What would he say when he discovered that she was pregnant? How would he react to knowing that she'd concealed it from him and, as far as he was concerned, might well have carried on concealing it unless he'd sought her out?

Could fate be so cruel as to offer her everything her heart desired in one hand, only to yank it back with the other?

'Shannon…' he murmured, his breath warm in her ear while his hand continued to caress her breast. Her nipples were erect, like soldiers standing to attention, and as he rubbed his thumb over the swollen bud protruding through the lace in her bra she knew that he could feel it.

Shannon took a deep breath. 'Look, there's something else I have to tell you,' she said awkwardly.

'Something else? Apart from your declarations of undying love? Now, what could that be, I wonder?'

'I can't think straight when—' She gasped as his wandering hand left her sensitive nipple to sweep beneath the hem of her dress. Just as well the car had been parked away from any streetlamps. He pressed his palm between her thighs and she squirmed against the steady, hard pressure, rubbing herself against him with half-closed eyes.

'When you're turned on?'

'Yes,' she said unsteadily. Her breathing sounded thick. 'And we can't do this here…'

'Then let's go back to my hotel room.'

'What would Mum say if she found out?'

'Why would she find out? I'll make sure to deliver you back safe and sound before the cock crows.' He laughed at the unwitting suggestiveness behind his remark. 'So tell me what you have to tell me.'

'I'm…'

'Yes?'

'I'm…' She tried desperately to recognise the importance of what she was about to say, but her mindless body was too busy responding to his hand which pressed rhythmically against her tights, already dampening at the erotic contact.

'You're not pregnant by any chance, are you?' He detached himself from her and tilted her face to his. 'Is that the revelation? That you're carrying my baby?'

She nodded mutely. 'And now you're going to walk away, aren't you? You're angry with me for not telling you sooner, aren't you? I don't blame you,' she cried, agonised, 'but what was I supposed to do? When I found out, the only thing I could think of doing was running away as fast as my legs could take me. And don't tell me that running away never solved anything!'

'I don't have to tell you, Shannon. I think you've discovered that all by yourself. And as for being angry with you, well, I wondered when you were going to tell me.'

Shannon looked at him in bewilderment. 'You *knew*?'

'I suspected,' he answered drily, and when she didn't say anything, he continued, 'I'm not a fool, my darling. I can add up as good as the rest of them, and I worked out that you hadn't had a period for well beyond the normal limits.'

'Why didn't you say anything?'

'Because I wanted you to,' he said simply. 'When you left, my first urge was to rush up here and confront you with it, but I knew what would happen. You would back off like a scared rabbit, and then, if I told you that I wanted to marry you, you would jump to the conclusion that I was proposing for all the wrong reasons, that I just wanted to fulfil my responsibilities. So I lost sleep for three nights and told myself that it was for the best because it gave you time to think. And then I told you how much I loved you because, my darling, I can't bear the thought of not being with you. Night and day. And the fact that you're having my baby is the icing on the cake.'

'It is? Am I dreaming?'

'If you are then so am I. Shall we continue with our pleasant little dream…in a hotel not a million miles away?'

At four in the morning, her body still tingling from hours of love-making, Shannon crept into the dark house, feeling like an adolescent terrified of being caught in the act of disobeying parental orders.

Kane would be coming around later that morning and she had made him promise to let her do all the talking.

'My mother might have a heart attack if she knew what we were up to,' Shannon had said to him. 'I don't think she suspected for a minute that you were anything but a nice man who had my welfare at the top of his mind.'

'Which I was,' he'd pointed out, as he'd stroked her thighs, his fingers as delicate as butterflies brushing against her skin. 'A kind hearted gentleman innocently taken advantage of by a wanton and abandoned young woman with a fabulous body and eyes that could drive a man crazy.' When he'd said that, his strolling fingers had begun stroking the bulging nub that made her groan in anticipated ecstasy, spreading apart her legs in eager arousal, and that had been the last coherent sentence for a while.

She hoped, as she surfaced from a dreamless sleep at ten o'clock that morning, that he remembered her instructions to leave the talking to her.

At ten-thirty, she rushed to answer the door and flashed him a warning look with her eyebrows.

'Don't forget,' she whispered, 'let me handle this.'

From behind his back he produced a startling bunch of lilies with the flourish of a magician pulling a rabbit from a hat.

'For me?' Shannon beamed.

'For your mother, actually,' he replied gravely, and she giggled behind one hand.

'Creep. Anyway, I've managed to clear the house of children and family, apart from Mum. I thought you might get distracted by lots of—'

'Computer-crazy adolescents?' He grinned and kissed her lightly on her lips. 'Mmm. Slightly swollen lips. Do you think it's the pregnancy or an overdose of love-making?'

'Shh!' Shannon laughed and dragged him through to the sitting room.

'Mum!'

'Well, Kane, I thought you might have been on a flight back to England. Come and sit down for a moment. I'm taking a rest from Christmas preparations.' She patted the chair next to her, flushing when he handed her the flowers. 'So, did you two children have a good time last night?' She looked shrewdly at her daughter. 'You must have. You didn't get back until well past three.'

'How did—?'

'Having children makes light sleepers of us all, Shannon. I take it the restaurant was an all-night one?'

'Well…' She glanced helplessly at Kane who smiled serenely back at her.

'We…have something to tell you, Mum.' Shannon reached out for the flowers and placed them on the coffee-table, then she sat down, leaning forward with her elbows on her knees.

'I'm sure you do. When is it going to be?'

'We haven't set a date as yet,' she said, gaping in disbelief.

'I didn't realise,' her mother said, frowning, 'that you could set a date for a birth. Technology must really have advanced without me noticing.' Then she saw her daughter's expression and laughed.

'I knew the minute you came back all in a rush, my girl, that you were in the family way. Just as I knew the minute I saw the both of you together that you were in love. There was no point in preaching to you about saving yourself for the right man because you'd found the right man and I expect you'll be married. *Won't you?* So. Where's the good in giving long lectures and trying to bolt the stable door after the horse has gone? Just tell me, how long have I got to do my knitting? And how much time do I have to look for a suitable hat?'

EPILOGUE

'YOU are the most exquisite creature in the world.'

Shannon looked drowsily at Kane and smiled. She watched as he tenderly picked up the eight-pound-three-ounce baby girl sleeping in the crook of her arm and watched as the tiny newborn figure stirred and stretched with closed fists and made small gurgling sounds before settling back into her new sleeping position.

She felt as fragile as a piece of china, Kane thought as he circled the small hospital room with his baby in his arms. A family. Eleanor, Sophie, Shannon and himself. Nothing else mattered.

For years work had been his driving force but now that he'd delegated much of it to his various directors it seemed natural to slide into a less frantic schedule. In a short while he would drive back to the house to collect Eleanor so that she could meet her sister for the first time, and as soon as Shannon was ready they would be moving out to the country and leaving London to the Londoners. He looked at his wife and felt a burst of gratitude and love.

'Have you called everyone on the list?' Shannon asked, and he went to sit by her on the side of the bed.

'You forget that you're speaking to the most organised person in the world.'

'Oh, is that right? Would that be why you forgot my overnight bag when I went into labour?'

'Ah, but you have to admit that I made sure it was packed weeks in advance.'

'How was Mum?'

'A bag of nerves,' Kane said drily, 'as you can imagine. They're all coming over tomorrow, so expect a hectic day of showing off our daughter. Your mother will be in her element considering you deprived her of a big, white wedding...'

'My mother has ample opportunity for big, white weddings with my sisters. Not that she's a big, white wedding kind of lady. Anyway, she said that she couldn't have hoped for anything more. Family only for the register office and then a reception in the grandest hotel in Dublin...'

Shannon closed her eyes and knew that even if the photographer hadn't been present, recording everything from every angle, she would still hold that memory in her heart for the rest of her life. The joy as she'd turned to Kane and kissed him chastely for the first time as his wife, her mother dabbing her eyes with a handkerchief, Eleanor bursting with the thrill of it all, and then the reception in Dublin where every friend and relative had showed up with good wishes on their lips.

She'd had her cream silk dress dry-cleaned and one day soon she would sit Eleanor down and tell her how much it meant to her, how powerful a symbol it would always be of her great happiness. When she looked at Kane, she saw him smiling at her, understanding what was going on in her head, the way he always did.

He placed the baby back with Shannon and watched in fascination as Sophie uncurled her fists and wriggled about. 'Now, reds, I feel you should get some rest before Eleanor comes to visit.' He leant over and kissed her on the tip of her nose. 'She's bursting with excitement at the thought of seeing you and our baby. Not forgetting your family...'

'They did kind of adopt her, didn't they?'

'They certainly did, Mrs Lindley.'

'Mrs Lindley.' She savoured the words and smiled at him. She wondered whether it would take her a lifetime to adapt to the fact that dreams could come true.

'My Mrs Lindley.' He raised her hand to his mouth and kissed it. 'And I would be no one without you.'

'Good,' she said comfortably. 'Because you're always going to have me.' She kissed their baby's downy head and thought how their love would only grow stronger over the years, a safe, secure haven she would never leave.

Coming
Next Month...

A special promotion from

Seduction and Passion Guaranteed!

Details to follow in September 2002
Harlequin Presents books.

Don't miss it!

The world's bestselling romance series.

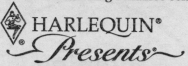

HARLEQUIN®
Presents

Seduction and Passion Guaranteed!

A new trilogy by **Carole Mortimer**

BACHELOR
COUSINS

Three cousins of Scottish descent—they're male, millionaires and marriageable!

Meet Logan, Fergus and Brice, three tall, dark, handsome men-about-town. They've made their millions in London, but their hearts belong to the heather-clad hills of their grandfather's Scottish estate.

Logan, Fergus and Brice are about to give up their keenly fought-for bachelor status for three wonderful women. Laugh, cry and read all about their trials and tribulations in their pursuit of love.

Look out for:
To Marry McCloud
On sale August, #2267

Coming next month:
To Marry McAllister
On sale September, #2273

Pick up a Harlequin Presents novel and you will enter a world of spine-tingling passion and provocative, tantalizing romance!

HARLEQUIN®
Makes any time special ®

Available wherever Harlequin books are sold.

More fabulous reading from
the Queen of Sizzle!

LORI
FOSTER

with

Forever and Always

Back by popular demand are the scintillating stories of
Gabe and Jordan Buckhorn. They're gorgeous, sexy
and single…at least for now!

Available wherever books are sold—September 2002.

And look for Lori's **brand-new** single title,
CASEY in early 2003

HARLEQUIN®
Makes any time special ®

If you enjoyed what you just read,
then we've got an offer you can't resist!

Take 2 bestselling love stories FREE!

Plus get a FREE surprise gift!

The world's bestselling romance series.

HARLEQUIN®
Presents~

Seduction and Passion Guaranteed!

**Harlequin Presents®
invites you to escape into
the exclusive world of royalty
with our royally themed books**

By Royal Command

Look out for:
The Prince's Pleasure
by **Robyn Donald**, #2274
On sale September 2002

**Pick up a Harlequin Presents® novel
and you will enter a world of
spine-tingling passion and
provocative, tantalizing romance!**

Available wherever Harlequin books are sold.

HARLEQUIN®
Makes any time special ®

Coming Next Month

THE BEST HAS JUST GOTTEN BETTER!

#2271 AN ARABIAN MARRIAGE Lynne Graham
The first book in Lynne's Sister Brides trilogy, this story is
dramatic, passionate and deeply emotional—it has it all! When
Crown Prince Jaspar al-Husayn bursts into her life, Freddy realizes he
has come to take their nephew away. Refusing to part with the child
she loves, she proposes marriage to Jaspar!

#2272 ETHAN'S TEMPTRESS BRIDE Michelle Reid
The second Hot-Blooded Husbands book is a unique and
compelling story with vibrant characterization and hot, hot
sensuality! Millionaire businessman Ethan Hayes told himself that Eve
was a spoiled little rich girl, intent on bringing men to their knees. But
it was all he could do to resist the temptation....

#2273 TO MARRY McALLISTER Carole Mortimer
Read the final title in the Bachelor Cousins trilogy and witness
the Scottish hero trading his independence for romance!
Dangerously attractive Brice McAllister has been commissioned to
paint a portrait of supermodel Sabina Smith. Aware of their mutual
attraction, he moves the sitting to a romantic, remote castle in Scotland....

#2274 THE PRINCE'S PLEASURE Robyn Donald
Part of the miniseries By Royal Command, this book celebrates
our year of royalty with an exclusive wedding! Prince Luka of
Dacia trusts nothing and no one—least of all his unexpected desire for
Alexa. Torn between passion and privacy, Luka commands that Alexa
stay safely behind closed doors entirely for his pleasure....

#2275 THE HIRED HUSBAND Kate Walker
An unusual, fascinating and very sexy marriage-of-convenience
story. You'll love the gorgeous hero!
Sienna Rushford desperately needs to claim her inheritance—
but her father's will states she must be happily married! So she hires
Kier Alexander as a temporary husband—but Kier has a proposition
of his own....

#2276 THE NIGHT OF THE WEDDING Kathryn Ross
Best friends become lovers, in this enjoyable read with a sexy
hero and sparky heroine! When Kate asked Nick to pretend to be
her escort at a wedding he reluctantly agreed. But to his surprise the
pretense came easily. And as night fell the mood deepened into
something neither he nor Kate had ever felt before....

HPCNM0802